Steppin' Ou... Si...

Steppin' Out on Sin

Latrese N. Carter

www.urbanbooks.net

Urban Books, LLC
78 East Industry Court
Deer Park, NY 11729

ISBN 13: 978-1-60162-306-5
ISBN 10: 1-60162-306-2

First Trade Paperback Printing July 2011
Printed in the United States of America

10 9 8 7 6 5 4 3 2 1

Distributed by Kensington Publishing Corp.
Submit Wholesale Orders to:
Kensington Publishing Corp.
C/O Penguin Group (USA) Inc.
Attention: Order Processing
405 Murray Hill Parkway
East Rutherford, NJ 07073-2316
Phone: 1-800-526-0275
Fax: 1-800-227-9604

I dedicate this book to my great aunt,
Addie Ruth Anderson
December 10, 1925–September 5, 2010

**May your soul rest peacefully in
the bosom of the Lord.**

Acknowledgments

God is good! I thank Him for strength, guidance, and the undeserved grace and mercies in my life! I feel an overwhelming sense of gratitude to have my fourth novel published. This has truly been a wonderful and blessed experience for me.

As I continue this literary journey, I would like to thank the following for your unwavering love, support, encouragement, prayers, and for believing in me:

My family, friends, literary agent, fellow authors, my wonderful freelance editor, publishing company, book clubs, bookstores, book sellers, distributors, librarians, and, last but not least, the readers. I am grateful for the new and faithful readers.

I'd like to give a special thank you to those who helped me as I wrote this book under an extreme amount of pressure and found my creativity stifled: Reginald C. Carter, Mary E. DeLoatch, Derek B. Stewart, Sr., Jada Thomas, Nikki Burns, and Aleisha LaChette. I cannot thank you enough for imparting your knowledge and imaginations to help me through the writing process.

Miss Reagan C. Carter, Mommy loves you!!!!

If I have spoken to you through any of my literary works, please feel free to e-mail me your thoughts at latrese@latresencarter.com. Also, visit my Web site at www.latresencarter.com.

Thank you and God bless,
Latrese N. Carter

Prologue

Jaime

Stunned. Confused. Disgusted. Fearful. Angry. Yes, all of these emotions I felt at once—all which had consumed me within seconds. Unable to close my mouth from the shock, I attempted to ask a few questions, but was speechless. What I wanted to voice only played out in my head. *Did she just say . . . Did she just confess to . . . Did I hear her ask for forgiveness for . . .* I closed my eyes tightly to block out the chaos around me. I had to attempt to make sense of this madness. I needed to replay it all to determine if I had actually heard what I thought I heard.

Pause. Rewind. Replay. Here I was, sitting in the New Year's Eve church service, waiting excitedly to ring in the year 2009 with my husband, Alonzo, my son, Isaiah, favorite cousin, London, my best friend, Riah, their husbands, and my loving church family. Our church, Spirit of Truth Ministries, always had the best Watch Night services. I always felt compelled to ring in the new year with God, and this year was no different. However, something had just gone terribly wrong.

As usual, the choir sang to the glory of the Lord, and there were multiple testimonies through the service, during which people sang hymns and praised God for all He'd done to sustain them throughout the year.

What was supposed to happen next was the sermon from our pastor. But someone had other plans.

Just before Pastor Steele could enter the pulpit to deliver his New Year's sermon, a young woman stood and asked if she could give her testimony. Of course, the theory in the Black church is that there's always time for one more person to speak, even when there really isn't. With the organist playing a soft rendition of "What A Friend We Have In Jesus," the congregation watched as this beautiful, tall, slim, middle-aged woman with long, curly, mixed-gray hair approached the microphone.

"Praise the Lord." She spoke in a sullen tone. "I'd like to give all praise and honor to our Lord and Savior for keeping me. He's been better to me than I've been to myself, and I just want to thank Him for His Grace and His mercy." The woman crossed her arms in front of her chest and rubbed her arms as if she were freezing cold. When she spoke this time, her voice trembled. "See, church, I'm a sinner. I found myself deep in sin that I had never envisioned. However, I was at such a low point in my life, I was vulnerable to anything and everything that came my way." She paused. "I'm not making excuses for my behavior, because I know right from wrong, but I have asked God to forgive me, and I am standing before you today to ask that you forgive me as well."

I looked over at Alonzo, bewildered, then at London, who shared the same look. What in the world was this lady talking about? Who was she? Why would she be asking us as a church to forgive her? Why would she need forgiveness from a bunch of strangers? This whole scene was a bit bizarre.

"Church, I . . . I ask that you forgive me for having a sexual affair with your pastor," she cried.

An array of noises flooded the sanctuary at once. I heard gasps and squeals and screams and cries of pain. But the woman continued to talk over the ruckus.

"You're a liar," bellowed one of the ushers from the back of the church. "And a harlot!"

The woman's demeanor instantly changed after hearing words in defense of Pastor Steele. Initially, she seemed to be begging for forgiveness. Now, it was apparent that she was fuming—so much so that she turned her testimony into a mission to air out all of our pastor's dirty laundry.

"I am not a liar!" she defended herself. With her neck rolling from side to side, she exclaimed, "I'm so sorry to tell you all, but your pastor is a fraud. Before you go into the new year listening to this man spew the Gospel, which he doesn't live by, I have to let you know the truth. For the past year, I've traveled with this man out of town to all his preaching engagements. When he's not traveling and not at the church, he's with me, at my house, in my bed, and lying to his wife about being at the church."

This woman was on a seething rampage now. Being called a liar fueled her fire. I was horrified as I continued to listen to this trollop's rant.

"I've had every kind of sex that you could ever imagine with this so-called man of God. Ask the good reverend about our foreplay and masturbation sessions and how he likes fingering me and putting his fist in my vagina."

There was instant wheezing and gasping throughout the sanctuary. Was this woman really standing in front of the church body talking about her vagina? Really? But her rant wasn't done with her illicit sex talk.

"Ask him if I'm lying about missionary sex, oral sex, anal sex, raw sex, yes, unprotected sex, and his pleas to have me involved in a threesome. Question your sex-crazed pastor about that strap-on he purchased and liked for me to use . . ."

The Jezebel's "testimony" time had ended. Two of our bodybuilder-like deacons came rushing to the front of the church to end this woman's tirade. They lifted her from her feet and proceed to remove her from the sanctuary. She kicked and screamed as she was carried out. "Get your hands off of me," she pleaded while punching one of the deacons repeatedly. "You can't stop me from telling to truth. I have proof—lots of proof. I have ticket stubs. I have receipts. I have voice mail messages. I have videotapes. You all will see. You'll see. I am not a fraud. Pastor Wesley Steele is the liar, and may God strike him dead for what he's done to me."

Finally, the deacons were successful in their quest to remove the woman from the sanctuary, but all was not well. She had created utter chaos within our church home. I looked over at First Lady Steele, the pastor's wife, who was surrounded by several members of the church. She looked as if she was having a panic attack. My heart immediately ached for her. No one should ever endure such public humiliation.

My eyes searched the pulpit for Pastor Steele. He was not there. His delayed entry into the sanctuary after the testimony portion of the service had been in his favor. He never witnessed any of the madness.

After trying to digest all that happened, I sat numb. I couldn't fathom any of that being true about *my* pastor. That kind of stuff happened in other churches, with other church leaders, but not *my* church. I just wanted Pastor Steele to come into the pulpit, denounce the vicious accusations, and bring forth the Word of the Lord for the new year. I was definitely ready to leave the drama in 2008.

With the church still in an uproar, I gathered that most people were in support of Pastor Steele. However, my husband, Alonzo, believed every word that came out of that tramp's mouth.

"Jaime, let's go home," he whispered in my ear for the tenth time. He was visibly disconcerted by the foolishness we'd just witnessed. I begged him to allow us to stay, to see how things would play out.

"Okay, Jaime, but only a few minutes more," he reluctantly agreed.

"Spirit of Truth family, may I have your attention please?" Minister Western asked. He was one of Pastor Steele's best friends in the ministry. "The devil is busy, but he's also a liar, and as a family, we will not let lies and fabricated stories disrupt our church home or our Watch Night service. Now, Pastor Steele is undoubtedly upset by these allegations and wants to spend some time with his wife and family to discuss this matter privately. However, we came here to praise God for 2008 and thank Him for blessing us to see 2009! Please bow your heads with me while I pray a special prayer for our pastor, his family, and for our church family. Let us pray."

I couldn't pray. I wanted to, but couldn't. I was quite perturbed that Pastor Steele had sent Minister Western to speak on his behalf. Why couldn't he have come out to address us directly? Of course, I understood being upset. Hell, we all were, but as the leader of Sprit of Truth, he had an obligation to say something.

With my head bowed, my eyes wide open, and my right leg shaking, I had many thoughts running through my mind about this entire situation. I couldn't get the woman's words out of my head about Pastor Steele and his various sex positions. Who would want to hear that about their pastor? Gross. *Can any of this be true? Did my pastor really have an affair with this floozy?* I had planned to reserve judgment until I knew all the facts. I truly hoped this was the work of Satan, and not God exposing a wolf in sheep's clothing.

I sincerely hoped that with the new year only thirty minutes away, the events and drama that had taken place at church were not a forewarning of what to expect in the coming year.

Chapter 1

Three weeks after that dreadful New Year's Eve service, I was still engulfed with skepticism about the validity of that bold confession given by that strange woman about Pastor Steele. Today would be my first Sunday back in church since then. I had received word from my cousin, London, that Pastor Steele would be in Sunday morning service and would finally address the rumors. I was a bit perturbed that it had taken this long for him to speak out about the scandalous accusations, but at least he was willing to do it.

I stared out my living room window. It had the makings of a cold January morning outside: no sun in the sky, leafless trees, and the cars in the driveway were covered with frost. The weather forecaster was calling for a dusting of snow, but this service was too important to miss. No matter the weather, I would be front and center, nestled into my favorite pew with my ears attentively listening to every word my pastor had to say. See, I still believed in him, despite what others may have said, and until I found out differently, I would not believe that stranger's admission of an affair.

"Good morning," Alonzo said as he descended into the living room.

"Morning."

"I see you're up early. Are you still going to church?"

"Yeah, babe. Gotta hear what Pastor Steele is gonna say to the congregation this morning."

Alonzo smirked. "I can tell you what he's gonna say. He's going to deny, deny, deny. That man knows the church is his bread and butter. He ain't gonna admit to nothing that's gonna mess up his paper. Believe that."

"Oh, Alonzo. Must you be so negative about this? You know this is killing me to have to deal with these God-awful allegations about him. Have some compassion. Be considerate of my feelings for once," I snapped.

"Stop overreacting. I am being considerate of your feelings. What you don't like is that I'm not telling you what you want to hear. You want me to hop on your bandwagon and agree that I think these rumors are false. I don't. I think he slept with that woman, and I don't think she's the only one. I think he's a fraud just like she described, and now his indiscretions have come to light. Sorry you can't see that, but I can."

I was hurt. Alonzo knew that I cared deeply for Pastor Steele. I had known this man for ten years. I had become a member of Spirit of Truth when I was twenty-three years old, after hearing Pastor speak at a women's conference held at my childhood church, where my parents were still members to this day. I was so moved by his message and how the Lord used him that I decided to branch out on my own and join a new church.

Pastor Steele had been like my spiritual father. He had always been there to guide me through the hard times, to share his wisdom, to counsel, to impart the Word of God, and to encourage me when needed. There were times I shared things with him that I never shared with anyone else. Pastor Steele had married Alonzo and me, and baptized Isaiah three years ago on his thirteenth birthday. He was a trusted confidant, and I had grown to love him like my own father. So, I absolutely disagreed with Alonzo.

"You're pissing me off, early on a Sunday morning. How about we just not talk about this? We don't see eye to eye. Fine. Believe what you want. I couldn't care less what you think about Pastor Steele."

Alonzo chuckled. "You mad? I struck a nerve, huh? Can't talk about the right reverend or you get all in a huff. Look, he's no different than me. He's a man, just like me. He puts on his pants, just like me. He went to college, just like me. He stands up to pee, just like me. He's no better and no different. So, you go on and get dressed for church, and get yourself all set up to listen to the bogus words coming from the false prophet, and I'll stay home and enjoy the AFC Championship Game. I'm out."

"Ugh!" I screamed as Alonzo walked back upstairs with his newspaper in hand.

My husband, Alonzo Clarke; I loved him. I really did, but he irritated the hell out of me sometimes. Alonzo never missed a moment to test how much I really loved him. At times, his arrogance was overbearing, and he was such a know-it-all, with his opinion and ideas always being the best.

Alonzo and I had been together for seventeen years. We met in high school during our junior year. During our high school days, Alonzo was well-liked among the girls. He was the popular, tall, athletic, muscular jock who was a member of the track and field team. His coffee complexion and smooth skin made all the young teen girls want to drop their panties. However, he shunned those girls and focused his attention on me. He claimed that I was different.

We met in a trigonometry class. He thought I was smart and always wanted to copy my homework. I thought he was cute, so I let him. Alonzo said that he was attracted to me because I seemed to genuinely like

him for him and not because he was an athlete. That
was true. I didn't care about track and field, or any
sport. I was all about my school work.

After weeks of "homework help," telephone conversations, and flirty smiles at school, we decided to make
it official. We were a couple. If looks were bullets, I'd
be dead. I was the most disliked teenager at the high
school, especially among the cheerleaders and sport
groupie-type girls, but I didn't care. It only made me
switch my hips down the hallways a little harder, and
give Alonzo more public displays of affection to make
them angry.

Alonzo and I attended the junior prom together. The
original plan—the plan we told our parents—was that
we were attending an after party at a friend's house,
but we had a different itinerary. When the prom ended
at midnight, instead of going to the after-prom celebra-
tion with our friends, we snuck over to the apartment
of Alonzo's older cousin, Romeo. Romeo was the cool
off-the-hook cousin who allowed the youngsters in the
family to come over his place to drink, smoke weed,
and party. On prom night, Alonzo and I headed to Romeo's house to roll around in the sheets. A month later,
I found out that I was pregnant.

The worst fear I could ever remember enduring was
having to tell my parents that at sixteen years old I
was pregnant. Not only did I expect the news to kill
them, I expected them to kill me and the unborn baby.
Together, Alonzo and I sat in the living room of my
parents' house and broke the news. "Crushed," "disappointed," and "hurt." I remember those words verba-
tim. "This is not what we wanted for you, Jaime. You're
so close to graduating from high school and attending
college." The looks on their faces were heart-wrenching. The news of the pregnancy was a colossal letdown.

Alonzo told his parents without me. They, too, were disheartened; however, they, along with my parents, agreed to support us in any way they could with raising the baby. In the middle of my senior year, I decided that it didn't make sense for both Alonzo and me to give up on our dreams of college. I helped him write his essays and send off his applications, and we hoped he'd get accepted into a great college that would help him achieve his dreams of becoming a lawyer.

At the end of senior year, our baby boy, Isaiah Jamal Clarke, was three months old. Two months later, in August, Alonzo left for Morehouse College in Atlanta, Georgia—a long way from our home in Alexandria, Virginia. I, on the other hand, stayed at home with my parents to raise Isaiah, giving up my hopes and dreams of pursuing higher education.

Four years later, when Alonzo graduated with his bachelor's degree, he attended law school in Washington, DC at Georgetown University. Law school was closer to home, and Isaiah got to spend more time with his father; however, the demands of the academic workload didn't allow Alonzo to be as involved in our lives as we had hoped. The distance and lack of quality time caused a lot of friction in our relationship. It was a hard seven years. I basically raised Isaiah by myself. I think I also harbored a little bitterness for not being able to follow some of my dreams earlier in life. At thirty-three years old, I often felt it was too late.

Finally, one year after law school, passing the bar exam, and obtaining a job as an attorney with the U.S. Department of Justice, Alonzo and I married.

It took no time for Alonzo's career to blossom, and it seemed that our lives were beginning to become comfortable. We moved to an upscale neighborhood— Mount Vernon Estates—where we purchased an enor-

mous five-bedroom single-family home. Two luxury
vehicles were parked in our driveway—Alonzo's Range
Rover and my BMW X5. We ate at the finest restaurants, and attended several balls, galas, and banquets
in the DC, Maryland, and Virginia areas, rubbing el-
bows with many political and celebrity figures. We had
a wonderful, talented, intelligent son, who attended
one of the most prestigious high schools within the
Fairfax County Public Schools system.

With all of Alonzo's success, we managed to stay
pretty grounded. We didn't walk around like snobs, nor
did we have inflated egos. We always remembered the
struggle from which we came.

Many had remarked that I made out well for standing by my man all those years and putting my life on
hold to allow Alonzo to pursue his dream and create
such a wonderful life for Isaiah and me, but they were
basing my success on materialistic items. I enjoyed
finer things; however I'd have taken peace and happiness any day over the money, the house, the cars, and
the events. I couldn't have cared less about worldly
objects.

See, on the surface it seemed like all was well in the
Clarke household, but it wasn't. All wasn't what it seemed
inside our four walls.

I took a long, hot shower. I prepared for church,
listening to some of my favorite gospel tunes on Praise
104.1. I sat down at the vanity in my bathroom and
looked into my sad brown eyes. I closed them. My heart
was heavy about the circumstances surrounding Spirit
of Truth and the lack of support I was getting from
Alonzo.

I began to apply concealer and foundation to my
face, using a makeup sponge to cover my cinnamon-
colored skin. Within the last few weeks, my face had

broken out with acne. No doubt this was stress related. With anxiety deep within about the church service, I tried to concentrate as I traced my eyes with eyeliner and enhanced my long lashes with mascara. I forced a smile to apply blush to the apples of my cheeks. Lastly, I pulled out my favorite M•A•C lip gloss and moistened my slightly plumped lips.

I walked out of the master bathroom and into the bedroom to get dressed. Just as I was about to slide my skirt up on my size-ten, curvy hips, Alonzo entered the bedroom.

"Sweetheart. I'm sorry about our earlier conversation. I should be more understanding. I know this is a rough time for you, and I haven't really shown compassion. I hope you get the answers you seek today, and I look forward to you coming home with some good news this afternoon about Pastor Steele."

"Thanks, Alonzo." I gave a half smile. "I appreciate your apology." I had to admit, I accepted his apology, but I was still a little sour about his earlier comments. I turned to the oval oak mirror hanging on the bedroom wall. I removed the black satin bonnet from my head and allowed my long, sandy-brown curls to fall to my shoulders.

"I asked Isaiah if he was going to church with you today, but he decided against it. Under the circumstances, I hope you don't mind if he stays home with me."

"No problem. I wouldn't want him to bear witness to any more church drama. I'd rather walk into Sodom and Gomorrah alone than to have my child exposed to it. So, I'm in agreement that Isaiah should stay home today."

"Well, be careful driving. The weatherman is calling for snow."

"I know. I heard it's supposed to snow. I'll be home right after church."

After our brief conversation, I gently kissed Alonzo on his cheek and told him I'd see him later. I was off to face Pastor Steele, who undoubtedly had some serious explaining to do.

Chapter 2

"Hey, cuz."

"Hey, Jaime. Thanks for pickin' me up for church this morning," London said.

I had called London prior to leaving home for church to ask if she would ride with me, since Alonzo and Isaiah weren't accompanying me. "No, thank you for agreeing to ride with me. For some reason, I didn't want to take this journey alone, and once I knew I didn't have the support of Alonzo, I knew I could call on you to support me."

London shook her head. "Chile, I think me, you, and Riah are going to have to uplift one another through this whole church ordeal. You see Nick isn't with me this morning either, and when I spoke to Riah, she said Everett wasn't going to be attending service either."

I chuckled. I wasn't surprised at the attitudes of London's husband, Nicholas, or Riah's husband, Everett. They shared the same sentiments as Alonzo. In the many conversations we'd had since the drama unfolded on New Year's Eve, they had all expressed their displeasure in the scrutiny surrounding Pastor Steele. However, they were a little gentler than Alonzo when expressing their thoughts about the situation.

"I hope you don't mind, but I called Riah and told her that we'd be riding together and offered her a ride—in your car." She laughed.

"Girl, you know that's not a problem. We've always been there for one another. Today is no different."

That was such a true statement. London Reed and my closet friend, Riah Mason, meant the world to me. We were stuck together like Super Glue. I was not sure how I would've made it through many of my difficult days without them by my side.

London was my first cousin. Our mothers were sisters who had a strong sibling bond. London and I followed in the footsteps of our mothers. We were extremely close. Although London was two years older than I, she and I were both only children and had been raised together like sisters. I had always looked up to her and admired her tenacity, strength, and determination. Even though she was petite in stature at five feet five inches tall, she always had big dreams and never let anyone or anything stand in her way.

At age twenty-one, she shocked the family when she announced after her undergrad graduation that she was marrying her college sweetheart. A few months later, she was pregnant with her son. Times were hard for London and Nicholas in the beginning of their marriage and people doubted that they'd endure the tough times. As Nick entered law school, London entered graduate school to obtain her degree in speech pathology, and they had a new bundle of joy to nurture. However, as a couple, and with the help of family, they endured and did well for themselves. Currently, Nicholas worked in a private practice, and London enjoyed being a wife, a mother to a teenage son, and a speech therapist in the public school system.

Not only was London a part of my family, but she was a trusted confidant and friend.

When we pulled into Riah's driveway, she was already standing behind the storm door, waiting for us to arrive. London and I laughed as she rushed to the car, wrapped in an abundance of winter gear: long wool trench coat, scarf, hat, earmuffs, and gloves.

"Is she going to church or skiing?" London joked.

Riah dove into the car, shivering. "I know y'all laughing at me. I don't care. It's cold."

"Yes, we were," I confirmed. "How long is the walk from your front door to the driveway? Dang. You'd think you were about to walk a mile the way you're all covered up."

"Look at my nose," Riah said, pointing at the tip of her nose. "It's red. That means it's cold."

"Um, Riah, you're high yella. Of course your nose is gonna be red. It doesn't take much for you to turn into Rudolph the Red-Nosed Reindeer."

Riah sucked her teeth. "Forget y'all. Betta be lucky we're on our way to church, 'cause I'd give you two a piece of my mind," she teased with her deep, raspy voice.

When people heard Riah speak, they were instantly shocked by her tone of voice because it didn't match her physical appearance. Being of mixed heritage, Riah was breathtakingly beautiful. Her mother was Korean, and her father was African American. Although she had many physical features of her father—tall, slim build, thick lips, and wide nose—her olive skin tone, long, straight black hair, and almond-shaped eyes were that of her mother.

Changing the subject, I said, "Speaking of church, what are your thoughts? London told me Everett didn't want to come today."

"Hell naw." Riah grabbed her mouth. "Forgive me, Lord. I mean heck naw. Everett said he doesn't even want to witness Pastor Steele's charade. He thinks it's all sickening, and he's been urging me to consider finding a new church home."

"Really?" London asked.

"Yes. He said that he can't ever see himself looking at the pastor the same again. And y'all know how much effort it took me to get Everett into church. Y'all remember when he used to say that anybody with the title reverend, minister, pastor, bishop, elder, or deacon was a jive-ass turkey." Riah slapped her lips. "O-M-G. What is wrong with my language this morning?"

London and I were cracking up at Riah.

"Anyway, I don't want Everett to get it in his head that all churches and pastors are the same. So, if he's still willing to attend church but prefers another place to worship, I may have to take him up on this, y'all. I gotta have my husband in church. Y'all no good, and, hell, well, me and my husband are bat shi . . . I mean, bat crazy, and we need Jesus. Damn Pastor Steele for screwing around with that lady. Did I just cuss again?"

I had tears forming in my eyes. Riah Mason was telling the truth. She was wild, but in a good way. She and I had been friends since the first day of ninth grade. We were both scared, unsuspecting freshman, who were overwhelmed by the size of our high school building. We leaned on each other to get through the first day of high school, and twenty years later, we were still each other's guide.

Riah came from a military background. Her father met her Korean mother while stationed in Taegu, South Korea. She had lived all over the world, including California, Hawaii, Germany, Arizona, and Georgia, and was extremely well-rounded. She worked as a radiologist and was a loving, giving person, but she had a fiery personality and just a wee bit of a potty mouth— even on a Sunday morning on her way to church.

"I feel ya, Riah. Depending upon what Pastor says today, Nick and I will be looking for a church home too."

"Let's not think the worst, you guys," I chimed in. "I'm still holding out hope that Pastor Steele will be able to shed a positive light on all of this. I promised I wouldn't judge or make any rash decisions until I heard from him. So, after today, I guess we'll all have our answers."

"I guess we'll see," Riah said from the back seat. "We'll see."

Chapter 3

The day after Pastor Steele's "forgiveness" sermon, I found myself struggling to abide by those words, especially coming from him. I wanted to believe in his innocence, but I needed something more from him—more of an explanation, more of an apology, more of something. That sermon, speech, or whatever it was he'd given yesterday just didn't cut it for me.

I hated that this Pastor Steele scandal had consumed me. I didn't sleep well. I constantly felt uneasy. The situation never left my mind. Nothing I did could take my thoughts away from it. I was a homemaker, so I didn't have a job to consume my time, or coworkers to chat with. Alonzo was at work. Isaiah was at school. London and Riah were tied up with their jobs. I just felt alone until my phone rang.

"Hi, Mommy," I whimpered.

"Hi, Jaime. Why do you sound like you lost your best friend?"

"Because I'm sad, Mommy. I'm really, really down today."

"Why, honey?" she questioned with concern.

"Because of all the stuff that's been going on at the church. My spirit is broken, Ma, and I feel so alone in all of this. London and Riah are leaving the church. Alonzo said he's never going back. I . . . I just don't have any support."

"Now, Jaime. You know as long as I have breath in my body, you have someone to lean on. Never think for a second that you're alone. My ears are here to listen, and my arms are here to hold you. I'm just a phone call or a drive away. Do you understand me?"

She was right. My mother, Paula Burke, was my rock. I knew I could always go to her with my problems, but sometimes I wanted to be an adult and attempt to handle things on my own. My mother encompassed such a nurturing, warm, loving nature. She had made it her life's mission to take care of me, my father, my son, the elderly, her church members, and the list went on and on. I just didn't want to lay my burdens on her because she'd already done so much for me.

My mother had worked as an occupational therapist with the elderly for many years, and then she retired two years ago. Most of her free time now was spent volunteering at adult day programs or assisted living homes, where the residents always described her as the little lady (being only five foot one) with a big personality and a big smile. As a faithful member of Morning Star Baptist Church of Christ, she spent many hours at the church, serving on several committees, including the missionaries, women's day, bereavement, hospitality, revival, church anniversary, and the building fund. Just recently my father and I teased her when she told us about the new group she joined, called the luau committee. I guess the church was planning a Hawaiian luau, and I was sure my mother had volunteered to roast the pig.

"I understand, Ma, I do, but sometimes I want to be a big girl, ya know? I don't want to call on you for everything."

"Jaime, I'm proud of the adult you've become. I know you're a woman, a very capable woman, so calling on me

when your heart is heavy doesn't change that. Why do
you think God gives us parents, siblings, spouses, and
friends? We're not supposed to be in this world alone,
enduring hardships. Now, I want you to remember that.
All righty?"

"Okay, Ma."

"So, I guess things with your pastor haven't gotten any
better, huh?"

"Not at all." I sighed. "Mommy, he was so intolerably
arrogant yesterday when addressing the congregation.
It was like he didn't care what had happened—like he
was mad at us for believing it."

"You're kidding."

"No, I'm not. It was the worst behavior I've ever witnessed from a man of God. I was highly disappointed
when I left."

"So, no admission, no denial, just 'y'all don't judge
me lest ye be judged' type of thing?"

"Exactly, Mommy. Then they played Donnie Mc-
Clurkin."

She laughed. "Oh, no, they didn't." Then she broke
out into the lyrics. "'For a *saint* is *just* a . . .'"

I, too, laughed. I was glad Mommy had helped me to
see some humor in this. "Ugh, I was so perturbed when
I left. It was just awful."

"Well, baby, you know I am not one to make decisions for you. But I want you to look at this entire
ordeal and see God in this. What exactly could He be
trying to show you? Where could He be leading you?
What could be His purpose in having you go through
this? I don't have the answers, so I can't tell you what to
do. But I can say lean not to thine own understanding,
and in all your ways acknowledge Him."

"What would you do, Ma?"

"Nope. I can't tell you that. I want you to seek God, listen to Him, and see what He tells you. Then let's chat again. Agreed?"

I huffed and reluctantly agreed.

"Oh, Jaime, before we go, your father wants to speak to you real quick."

"Did he hear you talking to me, Ma?"

"Sure did." She snickered.

"*Ma,*" I called out to her, but it was too late. She had passed the phone to my dad.

"Hello, Jaime," my dad said firmly.

"Hi, Dad. What's up?"

"What's up with you? I hear the mess is still brewing over there at your church."

"Yes, indeed. It's dreadful, Dad, and I don't know what to do. I'm confused and have no idea what to believe at this point."

"Well, unlike your mother, I'm gonna tell you how I feel. I understand seeking the Lord and all that, but let me give you some good ol'-fashioned advice."

My dad, Benjamin Burke, with a likeness to Berry Gordy, Jr., was a supportive family man. He was truly a devoted husband, father, and grandfather. He and Isaiah had the best relationship. Since he and my mother helped me to raise Isaiah, he often treated him like the son he never had. However, my father was also no-nonsense and could be quite blunt and direct. Sometimes his words, although truthful, could be abrasive, as he didn't believe in sugar-coating or softening his delivery.

Dad usually didn't get involved in drama, and especially not church matters, but he'd recently retired from the Washington Metropolitan Area Transit Authority (Metro), and had a lot more time on his hands to get involved in family issues. He had always been there for us when needed, but he spent a lot of time engrossed by his career. Now, having been retired for the last six months, he was spending more time at home, not waking up before 10:00 A.M., lounging on the couch, watching television, and going to the gym three times a week or out for an occasional walk or jog when it wasn't too cold. Unlike Mommy, he wasn't a frequent churchgoer. He loved the Lord, but proclaimed he didn't have to go to a building to worship Him. However, Daddy would attend church on special occasions such as Easter, Mother's Day, Father's Day, Church Anniversary, or anytime Mommy invited him. He never refused her request.

I was reluctant to speak with my father as I knew he was going to give me the uncut and raw version of his thoughts on the matter with Pastor Steele, and I wasn't sure I was ready. I braced myself.

"Okay, Dad. I'm listening."

"I know you're fond of Pastor Steele and that church. You've been there a long time. But, honey, where there's smoke, there's fire. Something in the milk ain't clean with that man. Ain't no woman in her right mind gonna stand up in front of a church full of people, with the first lady front and center, and confess to having a relationship with that man. And, from the way you tell it, she was by herself, no bodyguards, no entourage, no protection whatsoever. I don't think anybody is that bold to do such a thing based on a lie."

I sat quietly and listened with my eyes closed.

"The moment your mother told me what happened, I believed it, baby. Then I went to the gym, and guess who the talk of the town was? Pastor Steele. His business is all out in the open. People have been talking about this mess nonstop. It's not a good look for him, the church, or his family, and, quite frankly, I don't want you surrounded by that foolishness."

A teardrop fell from my eye. I knew without a doubt that my father was telling me the truth.

"Jaime, you're a grown woman and I can't tell you what to do," he continued. "But I want you to know that if I were you, I would want to disassociate myself from this. I mean, who really wants to attend church with this salacious gossip lingering in the air? How could you ever really focus on this man preaching the Gospel, all the while wondering about his guilt or innocence? It's too much of a distraction, if you ask me. And God ain't about no confusion. Again, do as you see fit, but I'm just telling you how I feel."

"Thank you, Dad. I appreciate your honesty."

"You're welcome. I love you. We'll talk to you later. Oh, and tell Isaiah to call me."

"Will do. Love you."

By this juncture, I had talked to Alonzo, London, Riah, and my parents. Now, it was time for me to seek the Lord. With the weight of the world on my shoulders, I fell to my knees. "Dear Lord . . ."

Chapter 4

After spending some quality time with the Lord in prayer, I decided to lie across my bed for a nap. I was tired. Sleep had escaped me the night before as I tossed and turned in the darkness. In the midst of some much needed rest, my house phone rang. I ignored it. It rang again.

"Ugh! I wanna sleep," I growled. I ignored it again.

Now my cell phone was ringing. By this time, my rest was totally disrupted and someone was trying to reach me. I reached for my BlackBerry and answered.

"Jaime, where are you?" London asked excitedly.

"I'm at home," I responded, my tone groggy.

"I've been calling you at home. Why didn't you answer?"

"Because I was asleep," I snapped. "What's up?"

"Girl, you gotta wake up and check your e-mail."

"What?" I was annoyed.

London demanded, "Check your e-mail—now!"

"Why?"

"Because you said you wanted proof about Pastor Steele and that woman, right? Well, honey, proof is circulating the Internet as we speak. I sent you a link in your e-mail, so get up and check it."

I sat straight up. London had finally gotten my full attention. "Are you serious? What kind of link? Do you mean more stuff from blogs and message boards? If so, I've read enough of that stuff already."

"Naw, honey. Just check your e-mail. I gotta get back to work, but we'll talk later. One piece of advice before clicking the link: have a brown paper bag beside you just in case you throw up. Love you. Bye."

Now, how is she gonna drop a bomb like that, and then rush off the phone? I walked into the computer room and logged in to my e-mail. There were fifteen new messages, all from different people with the same subject: FW: proof Pastor Wesley Steele cheats on wife. I clicked on the message from London. Just as she said, there was a link. I clicked the link. A new window opened and a video appeared. The name of the video was the same as the subject of the e-mail message. Before I pressed play, I observed a still screen of what appeared to be Pastor Steele with a woman, but the picture wasn't clear. I hit the play button and held my breath.

"Oh, my goodness," I yelled. My eyes were as big as tennis balls. My mouth went immediately dry; I couldn't clench my lips because of the shock. The volume on my PC was turned up, and the sounds coming from my speakers made the viewing experience even more sickening. The video started with a woman performing oral sex on a man who, without a doubt, was Pastor Steele. She made exaggerated slurping sounds while he pushed her head up and down on his manhood. I covered my eyes. I was horrified. This was a vision I never wanted to see.

I got up the nerve to spread my fingers apart and peek through them to look at the screen. The video cut to the two of them in a sixty-nine position, then cut to them beginning to have unprotected sex, just as the woman described, with Pastor slapping her butt as she called him "Big Daddy." There was a jump in the video. A new scene popped up. This time, Pastor Steele sat in

a chair. The harlot straddled and grinded on him as he
sucked and bit her breasts. Then she moaned, "Suck it,
Pastor. Suck it."

My stomach churned. I couldn't take it anymore. I
threw up in my mouth. I couldn't watch any more of
the vile, disgusting video. I had seen enough.

"That lying, cheating, so-called man of God. How
could he? How could he play with so many people's
lives?" I cried out. I was enraged. The man I looked
upon as a father, a spiritual advisor, was nothing more
than an adulterous whoremonger who was playing
church and playing with God. I instantly went from
loving this man to loathing him. He was a pathetic human being, and, in my moment of hurt, I wanted something extremely bad to happen to him.

I looked out the window of the computer room and
saw Alonzo's car pull up in the driveway. I ran to the
door. Before he could step foot in the door, I wailed,
"Alonzo, it's true. It's all true."

Confused, he asked, "What's true, Jaime?"

"All the stuff about Pastor Steele. He did have an affair with that woman. It's on video."

Alonzo reached out and held me in his arms. "Don't
cry, Jaime. I heard about the video. Everett called me
at work today and told me. I didn't watch it, but I heard
it's pretty graphic, and there's no doubt it's Pastor
Steele."

"Oh, it's him, and it's the hussy who stood up in
church on New Year's Eve."

"I know you didn't want to think the worst of him.
He let you down. He let a lot of people down. There
are a lot of hurt people at Spirit of Truth right now,
and he'll be held accountable for that. But I don't want
you wallowing in sorrow over this. You can and will
get through this. Just like you found this church, you'll

find another. Just know next time not to put your faith in man, 'cause man will let you down every time."

I pulled away. "What do you mean?"

"I'm just saying that when you search for a new church home, I wouldn't be so quick to develop a relationship with the pastor. Remember that he's a man, not the Messiah. He's bound to mess up and make mistakes. So I'd focus more on the Word of God than the messenger."

"How dare you say that to me?"

"Jaime, please don't take it the wrong way," Alonzo pleaded. "I don't mean it the way it sounds."

"Yes, you do. Why don't you just say, 'I told you so.' You wanna rub it in my face anyway, don'tcha?"

"No, I don't. I find no pleasure in that. All I'm saying is, now you know the truth. It's time to move on. Let's get past this, find a new place to worship, and, in our quest, let's try to focus more on God's Word than worshipping the man of God, because he has flaws."

"Worshipping? Worshipping? So, you think I was worshipping Pastor Steele?"

"Look, I can see you're really upset right now. I don't seem to be making things any better. I'm gonna head upstairs to change my clothes, and head out to hang out with Everett for a little while. Maybe we can talk later."

"If you have the same callous response, then, no, we can't talk. You just don't get it. I'm crushed behind this and your way to deal with it is to move on. Really? Whatever! Maybe if you went to church a little more, you'd understand."

"See, now you're being nasty for no reason. I'm not the enemy, Jaime. I didn't do it. My name isn't Wesley Steele. And until you get that straight, you're right; we have nothing to talk about regarding this. I'm not gonna be your verbal punching bag."

I rolled my eyes and walked away. To hell with Alonzo. He was such a loser when it came to supporting my needs. Instead of staying home and helping me deal with my anguish, he was going to hang out with friends. Typical Alonzo.

When he left, I called Riah and London to come over to sit with me, and they agreed. It was a damn shame that I had to lean on my friends to help me deal with this turmoil and not my husband.

Chapter 5

The first day of spring semester classes brought about renewed enthusiasm within me. Although it was a bone-chilling cold day in February, I was eager to get out of the house, mingle with other people, and get my mind off of all the Spirit of Truth drama.

Alonzo had been doing so well in his career as an attorney at the U.S. Department of Justice that we'd agreed I didn't have to work. However, I hated sitting at home by myself. Isaiah was no longer a little boy, the house didn't need cleaning every day, and I wasn't one to watch talk shows, court shows, and game shows all day long. So, to keep myself busy, I enrolled in classes through a program called Adult and Community Education (ACE), which was offered every semester by Fairfax County Public Schools. Some asked why I didn't take the time to go to college to earn a degree, but I often felt like I missed that opportunity; it just seemed too late to start a four-year program now. Besides, I didn't even know what I'd major in. Over the years, I thought I wanted to be a nurse, a psychologist, a social worker, or a teacher. Clearly, I was all over the place, so I just settled for being a housewife and taking classes through ACE. I was pretty much content at this point.

In the past, I'd taken many classes that I enjoyed, including floral design, international cooking, personal growth and mind development, CPR and first aid, nutrition, and various computer courses, my favorite being Web design. Today, I was embarking upon a new experience, one I was extremely excited about—digital photography. I was so thrilled about this class that as soon as I paid the tuition, I ran out and purchased a digital single-lens reflex camera—the type of camera the professionals use. Not only was I ready for a new experience, but I was in need of a distraction, something to take my mind off all the chaos that had been going on around me for the last month.

I arrived at the campus thirty minutes prior to class. When I walked into the classroom, I immediately spotted a familiar face. He noticed me too.

"Hi, Mario." I waved from across the room.

"Hey, Jaime," he said, rushing over to give me a hug. "How are you?"

I had to stand on my tiptoes when we embraced, because he was six foot two. "I'm okay. And you?" I said, staring at his smooth Nestlé dark chocolate skin and his dazzling Colgate smile.

"I'm well."

"Don't you look handsome? I see you cut your hair." I rubbed my hands in his low-trimmed hair. This was a change from the dreadlocks he used to wear.

"Yeah, new year, new look. I shaved the hair off my face, too."

"I see. I like the new look. Makes you look older," I teased.

"Please don't start with that 'young buck' stuff again. Anyway, so are we in class together again?"

"Looks like we are," I responded.

"Aw, hell. This professor better look out. The two of us up in here ain't nothin' but trouble," he joked.

I couldn't stop laughing. Mario Fox was my homie. He and I had taken several ACE courses together. We had become friendly, but never really friends outside of class. He was always such a joy to be around, so I was elated that he and I would be learning about digital photography together. As he was just twenty-five years old, I often referred to Mario as a young buck. He hated that because he was very mature for his age and extremely intelligent. Mario had obtained a degree in political science from George Mason University a few years ago, but refused to utilize his degree. He claimed that he only attended college at the insistence of his parents. He really just wanted to travel the world. Mario grew up in the affluent area of Fairfax County, where his neighbors were senators and congressmen. His parents were involved heavily in the political arena. Mario wanted nothing to do with that lifestyle. Although very knowledgeable about politics, he wanted to be more of a free spirit. He did what he wanted to do when and how he wanted to do it.

"There's a seat over by me. Let's chat before class starts," he said. I followed Mario to the table where he was seated, removed my coat, and sat across from him. "So, what's been going on with you lately? I guess I should say Happy New Year since this is the first time I've seen you."

"Happy New Year to you too. However, it hasn't been a happy year for me at all."

He frowned. "Why?"

In a whisper, not wanting other classmates all in my business, I said, "My pastor has been involved in a scandal since the beginning of this year, and now there's a videotape on the Internet of him sexing a woman who's not his wife."

"Get the hell outta here. Oh, my goodness. That's right. I forgot that you went to Spirit of Truth Ministries." Mario got all excited. I looked around the room because I didn't want anyone to know I was associated with that church.

"Shh. Damn, Mario."

In a lower tone, he said, "Oh, sorry. Didn't mean to put you on blast."

"So, you heard?

"Who hasn't? I even saw that nasty sex tape. Word is the woman put it out there because nobody believed her. I heard she was planning to send it to *The Washington Post* and to TV news outlets. That ho ain't playing."

"Now, why in the world would she need to go that far? That tape don't make her look no better."

"'Cause she ain't got nothin' to lose. And her purpose is to bring him down. What other way to do it than to expose him publicly?"

"This is such a travesty. Just downright sad." I shook my head. "I hate even talking about this 'cause it gets me so worked up."

"So, that's why you haven't been having a good year so far?" he asked with concern.

"Yeah. This year sucks balls already. I've lost my pastor, church home, faith in God, faith in church, faith in my husband's support—"

"Wait, wait, wait. Back up. Faith in God? Faith in church? Faith in husband's support? Elaborate, please."

"Well, after this, I cannot see myself ever going back to church. I don't think I'll ever trust another pastor ever again. Church hurt is the worst kind of hurt, and until you've endured it, you'll never know. My faith in God still remains. However, I do question how and why He would allow this to happen. Why He, all-powerful, all-knowing, would allow this man to affect so many lives so adversely? And, as far as my husband goes, he has not given me the support I expect him to give as I have suffered through this turmoil. He just doesn't get it. His answer to it is to move on, find a new church home, and next time don't worship the pastor."

"He said that?" Mario asked, surprised.

"Yeah, he made that ignorant-ass statement to me, and I'm still pissed about it."

"Wow. That was pretty insensitive."

"Damn right it was. I haven't had much to say to him since that conversation."

Mario reached across the table and grabbed my right hand. "Well, friend, I'm here for you if you need me. I may not have all the answers regarding church hurt, but if you need someone to talk to, I am readily available to help. Before we leave class today, I'll give you my e-mail address, and home and cell numbers. You can call me anytime, day or night, if you just want to talk."

"Aw, Mario. That's very sweet of you, but I can't ask you to do that," I said while gently sliding my hand out of his. It was a nice gesture to want to be a listening ear, but, in my eyes, he was a little boy. He hadn't lived long enough for me to lean on or listen to his advice. Even talking to him, I could smell Enfamil baby formula on his breath. Although it was very kind of him to extend himself, I wouldn't take him up on his offer.

Sadly, as I continued to talk to this young man about my feelings, the more I realized he was more in tune than Alonzo to how I felt. How a person, an associate, could be more compassionate than my own husband was baffling. Mario's kindheartedness only solidified my thoughts about Alonzo being a selfish bastard.

Chapter 6

Once class ended, I headed home to get an early start on getting dinner ready for Alonzo and Isaiah. I put three Cornish hens in the oven and began preparing rice and string beans to accompany the poultry.

While the food was cooking, I walked into the dining room and sat at the large oak dining table to go through the large stack of mail I'd brought in the house.

"New month, same bills." I sighed as I looked at the water, cable, telephone, gas, electric, and cell phone bills. I put the bills off to the side in their own pile to pay later. There were a few circulars and pizza delivery menus also included in today's mail. But there was one piece of mail that stood out because it wasn't a bill or junk mail. It was rather intriguing and caught my eye. This envelope, addressed to Alonzo, wasn't a bill at all. It was a pink business envelope with a scent. The sender's name was Candice Barr. I put that envelope to my nose and sniffed. "What the . . . This smells like perfume."

I started to feel uneasy. I wasn't really sure I could truly identify my feelings at this moment, but I just knew I didn't like what I was seeing. I flipped the envelope over on its backside and, to my surprise, there were two bright red lip prints.

"Aw, hell no! What in the he . . ."

I usually didn't open Alonzo's mail, but this piece of mail was highly suspicious. Hurriedly, I ripped open the envelope. Inside was a piece of flowery stationery with the name Candice Barr in script writing centered at the top. My eyes fells upon the words that were addressed to my husband:

> *My Dearest Alonzo,*
> *I hope this letter finds you finally at peace. I know these past few months have not been easy for you, as you have been enduring those God-awful divorce proceedings. I am elated that that part of your life is almost behind you, and we can finally move on with our lives. I hope that within these last nine months I have proven to be the woman you've always wanted. I promise that your new life with me will be more fulfilling than your previous marriage. I am counting down the minutes to when we can finally be together without hiding our relationship. I'm so ready to scream from the rooftop how much I love you. You are the kind of man I've yearned for all my life. You are my best friend, protector, supporter, provider, and absolutely the best lover I've ever had.*
> *It won't be long, baby, before it will be you and me forever. Until then, I'll be thinking of you and patiently waiting for you to be in my arms again. I love you, sweetie.*
> *Love Always,*
> *Your sweet, succulent Candy Barr*
> *P.S. Thanks so much for paying my rent this month. I don't know what I'd do without you.*

My heart stopped. The letter slowly drifted to the floor as I lost all feeling in my hands. I was dismayed, in disbelief at the words I had just read. I gradually be-

gan to feel my body tremble. I stood shaking for what
seemed like an eternity before I finally spoke.

"Oh my goodness," I sobbed. All these key words
from the letter were swirling around in my head. "Divorce? Nine months? Provider? Protector? Lover? Paying her damn rent? This muthafu . . ." I almost let the
word escape from my lips, but I caught myself. When
I gave up on church and faith after the Pastor Steele
scandal, sadly, I'd abandoned my Christian values, too.
The most noticeable change was my explicit language.
I was trying to control my use of profanity, but after
what I'd just read, I knew I was gonna give Alonzo a
tongue-lashing full of expletives. "He must've lost his
damn mind."

With all my might, I was trying to comprehend all
that I had just read. I couldn't see straight. I couldn't
think straight. The only thing that was clear and the
only thing that I could utter was, "He's doing it again?
He's doing it to me again?"

By "again" I meant the infidelity. Alonzo's cheating
ways were nothing new. Quite frankly, Alonzo was a
man whore. I didn't know it during our high school
days, but found out quickly during *his* college days and
the days to follow.

During undergrad, Alonzo was bumping and grind-
ing with every chick in Atlanta. I found out about a
couple while visiting him. He was too stupid to hide
the naked pictures of the girls in his dorm room with
handwritten messages on the back. One picture was of
a young coed with her vagina exposed that said, "This
is all for you." It was such a horrible feeling knowing
that I was at home raising our son while he was away
at school living the life and screwing every girl in sight.

Our relationship was strained and pretty much off
and on during his Atlanta days, but when he returned

home and went to law school locally, I felt a little more secure about us as a couple. Unfortunately, law school was no different. While I thought he was knee-deep in studying, he was knee-deep in some other woman's vagina. This was proven through archived messages that I found from reading his Yahoo! Messenger account. It seemed he was instant messaging one of his law school classmates, and they were much more than study partners. When I approached him with this, he denied a sexual relationship and agreed to stop being her "study partner." Like a dummy, I forgave him.

I'd gotten an e-mail from another woman, who attached a picture of herself and Alonzo with a caption that said, "Don't we look cute together?" His response to the questionable photograph was that she was a friend of a coworker who was out with them for a happy hour, was drunk, took the picture, and so forth. So, how had she gotten my e-mail address? I was still trying to figure that one out.

The last incident was about four years ago when I was doing laundry. I placed a pair of his jeans in the washer, and two condoms fell out of a pocket. He claimed that he had picked them up for Isaiah because he was planning to talk to him about protecting himself when he started having sex. Yeah, right. Alonzo was full of it.

The condom incident was the last of anything that had happened in a while, and although I had little to no trust in my husband, I had hoped that four years of no incidents meant that he had finally decided to grow up and be the man and husband God intended for him to be. It seemed I was sadly mistaken. The letter from Candice Barr confirmed he hadn't grown up one bit. He just *thought* he'd covered his tracks better.

Alonzo's lust for other women was downright despicable. So why did I marry him? I married him because I wanted my family to be whole. I wanted to raise my son in a home with his mother and father. It was my desire to live the all-American dream with the two-parent household and nice house with the white picket fence. Besides, I just kind of thought that once Alonzo started doing well for himself financially, I should've been the only woman reaping those benefits after all the hell I'd endured as his girlfriend, fiancée, and wife. I also expected that once Alonzo got older, he'd eventually get that lustful spirit out of his system and appreciate the woman he had at home. *Guess not,* I thought.

Pissed off, I started pacing in the kitchen. I searched my brain as to how I was going to handle this. Honestly, I wasn't up for the usual way I handled these matters. In the past, I'd question and he'd deny, even with proof staring him in his face. Lie and deny and use of the sharp lawyer tongue was how he attempted to get out of these situations. I just wasn't up for the normal song and dance. I was ready to rumble upfront and ask questions later.

I was just about sick of lying, cheating men. First, Pastor Steele had started off the year with his scandalous behavior, and now, a month later, Alonzo had brought this same garbage to my front door. I was so done with these deceitful-ass men. I wasn't even going to spend a ton of energy crying over this man whore anymore. It was time to wipe my tears and get even.

"I am gonna make this lying sack of shit wish he had never married me," I exclaimed.

I picked up the phone to call London. "Hey, cuz. Listen, I can't talk long. I can't give a lot of detail right now. I've got a little emergency. I'm okay. Nobody's hurt, nobody's dead. I just got something I need to handle. I need to ask a huge favor of you."

"Jaime, you're scaring me. What's going on?"

"Can't get into all of that right now," I said, panting. My blood pressure was rising with each passing moment. "Can you please pick up Isaiah from school after basketball practice for me, and take him to your house? I need to handle some things with Alonzo, and I don't want him here. I'll pick him up from your house when I'm done."

Hesitantly, she responded, "O . . . okay, Jaime, but I wish you'd tell me more."

"Will do when we talk later. Thanks, cuz. Love you. Gotta go."

When I hung up, I walked over to the stove. There would be no dinner in the Clarke household tonight. I turned off the burners and turned off the oven, but the Cornish hens remained. I spied my twenty-three-piece kitchen knife set. This set, comprised of a variety of knives and tools, could be used for cooking and many tasks in the kitchen. It was originally purchased after I'd taken my international cooking class. I walked over and removed the butcher knife. I smiled. There would be no cooking or kitchen tasks done with this knife today.

With case, I walked down the steps heading toward the basement. In the back of the basement was my least favorite room in the house—the laundry room. But, when I opened the laundry room door today, I beamed. My glee had absolutely nothing to do with laundry, but everything to do with that bottle of bleach I removed from the shelf.

With the bleach in one hand and the butcher knife in the other, I walked upstairs to the bedroom. No doubt, I was hurt by the content of Candice's letter, but more than sad, I was irate. I was tired of being used, misused, and abused. I had had enough. When Alonzo got home, I was going to introduce him to his new wife—a woman scorned.

Chapter 7

I was exhausted. My rage, coupled with the wrath I had just unleashed upon everything Alonzo owned, had worn me out. I leaned back against my bedroom wall, in the space between the bed and dresser. I tried to catch my breath. Slowly, I slid down the wall until my butt hit the floor. I needed to recuperate, as I was not done with Mr. Clarke. Since that whore Candy Barr had stated that Alonzo was planning to divorce me to be with her, I was going to make sure he had nothing to take with him. Everything he owned would be doused in bleach and destroyed, including clothes, shoes, and jewelry.

I inhaled and exhaled several times in attempt to calm myself. Just as I released the air from my lungs, I heard the front door open. Boy, was Alonzo in for a surprise.

"Jaime," Alonzo called from downstairs. I didn't answer. I continued to sit on the floor of our bedroom, twirling the butcher knife in my hand.

"Jaime," he bellowed. Still I didn't respond. I could tell by the tone of his voice that he'd been greeted by the not-so-pleasant odor when he entered the front door. I heard his footsteps as he began to climb the stairs, no doubt in an attempt to locate me.

"Jaime! Why does the house smell like bleach?" he yelled as he made his way down the hallway toward our bedroom. When he entered through the doorway of our bedroom, he stopped dead in his tracks.

"What the fu . . . ?" he mumbled. The look on his face was priceless. There was a mixture of concern and confusion. Then he noticed me in the corner of the bedroom on the floor with the knife.

"Jaime. What is going on in here? Are you okay?" He rushed toward me.

"Don't come near me, or I'll kill you," I roared.

He instantly stopped walking. "What's wrong? Why does our bedroom look like it's been ransacked? Have you been hurt?"

I gave a sinister grin. "Have I been hurt? Have I been hurt? Yes, I've been hurt."

"Okay. Let me call the police," he said while running over to the cordless phone on the nightstand.

"No need to call the police, 'cause if you do, you'll be calling on yourself or on me after I'm done with you."

With a look of uncertainty, Alonzo said, "Jaime, I'm not following you, sweetheart. Your words aren't making sense to me right now. I'm worried. If there was an intruder, I need to call the police. If you've been hurt, we need to get you help. Please, tell me what happened."

I stabbed the knife repeatedly into the carpet, then softly and slowly asked, "Who the fuck is Candice Barr?"

"Who?" Alonzo scowled.

"I'm going to ask you one more time, and if you act like you don't know who I'm talking about, I'm going to get up off this floor, and then the next thing I will stab will not be this carpet. Now, let's try this again. Who the fuck is Candice Barr?"

In a stutter, Alonzo responded, "She . . . she's someone who works in DC. Her agency does some work with the justice department. Why?"

Still very calm, with my eyes focused on the knife in my right hand, I asked, "So, you two have a working relationship?"

"I mean, I wouldn't call it a working relationship. I see her here and there. She's gone to a few happy hours with us after work, but other than that, that's it."

"You're a lying piece of shit, Alonzo, and you know it. Why don't you take a look at that letter on the bed? And then tell me if you can come up with a truthful answer about who Candice Barr is?"

Alonzo snatched the letter from the pink envelope. I watched as he read the letter line by line. I studied his face to see if his facial expression would change. His eyebrows raised a couple of times, but other than that, there was nothing really dramatic. Once done, he folded the letter, placed it back into the envelope, and said, "So, that's what all of this is about? You received some letter from this chick, who is obviously lying, and you have made our home smell like a janitor's closet with all this damn bleach. You've got our bedroom looking like a tornado hit it over this? You really believe this garbage?"

Did this Negro really just cop an attitude with me? Did he really? "Alonzo, you damn right I believe it. With your fucked-up track record of fidelity, or lack thereof, I'm not surprised by anything you do anymore. The only thing that surprised me was to read that we were divorcing. When were you going to tell me, you bastard?"

Alonzo shouted, "That's what I'm trying to get you to see. This bitch is making this shit up. Yes, I know her. But I ain't fuckin' her or paying her bills, nor have I told her I was divorcing you and going to be with her. She's delusional. This shit ain't true. Now, you all up in here pouring bleach all over my shit and cutting up my clothes for nothing." He held up one of his white dress shirts. "What the hell did you do to my shirts?"

"I cut the heart out of each and every one of them because you're one heartless son-of-a-bitch. You don't care about nobody but yourself, and you only think with the head between your legs. You never consider that your actions will hurt me or your son or anybody else around you. I'm sick of you, Alonzo. *Sick of you.*"

"This is just wrong, man! Just wrong. I know I've messed up in the past, but the stuff in this letter ain't true. What can I do to prove it to you? Do you want me to call my coworkers, Everett, Nick, anybody who can confirm that I've been walking the straight and narrow?"

"Do I look stupid to you?" I shrieked. "I don't want you to call anybody. Your history, your character, your lack of integrity, and your inability to be monogamous are enough for me. There's nobody you could call who could make this better for you."

Then a light bulb suddenly went off in my head. If Alonzo only knew this woman in passing, as a work associate, how and why . . . ? This made absolutely no sense to me.

"So, tell me this, Alonzo. You claim to only know this woman in passing, as a work associate. So how did she get our address? Did she just randomly pick a married attorney, who works at the justice department, seek out his address, and decide to send a letter to his home address for no reason at all? Does that shit make any sense to you?"

Alonzo seemed frustrated with trying to explain himself, but I didn't give a damn. Had he not put himself in this predicament, he would not be facing the firing squad right now.

"Like I said, I don't know what this woman's motives are. Honestly, I don't. All I can tell you is that I can look into it when I get to work tomorrow and try to figure out what's going on."

"When you get to work? Come on, don't you have her home or cell number programmed in your phone under some other name? I'm sure you can contact her now if you really wanted to. Hell, you're a lawyer. Don't you have investigators on speed dial? If you really wanted to get to the bottom of this, you'd do it now, not wait until tomorrow. But you and I both know you're full of shit."

"*Grr!*" Alonzo growled. "I'm not getting anywhere with you. No matter what I say, you're not gonna believe it. I'm wasting my breath here. I'm leaving!"

"Whatcha mean you leaving?" I jumped quickly from the floor, knife in hand.

"I'm gonna bounce before I do something I'll regret. Looking at my bleach-stained, cut up clothes is making me angry. The fact that you believe some deranged broad over me is pissing me off even more. There's nothing more I can verbally add to this conversation. So, before I take that knife out your hands and do some harm, it's best I leave."

With fury in my eyes, my heart seething, I snarled, "Look here, you bastard. I know this game. This argument is your escape. This is your chance to now turn to that heifer. I get it."

With the knife pointed directly toward Alonzo, I began walking in his direction. "Let me tell you one thing, Alonzo Clarke. She can have you! I'm so done. I'm done with your lies, your cheating, your deception, and being hurt by you."

At that moment, I was in attack mode. Once he said he was leaving, I just knew he was going to see that home-wrecking hussy, and that elevated my anger 100 percent. I was out for blood.

As I continued walking toward Alonzo, he began backing away, heading toward the bedroom door. "So if you wanna go be with that bitch, then go," I said. "You have my permission to do whatever it is ya wanna do. I don't give a fuck." And with that, just like in the *Psycho* movies, I raised the knife, lunged at Alonzo, and screamed, "Fuck you, fuck her, and fuck your life. I'm done with you."

Alonzo dashed out the bedroom door. He sounded like he tripped down the steps trying to get away from me. I missed him—on purpose. I was angry as hell, but not crazy. I had a son to think about, and I couldn't raise him from prison. However, I wasn't done with Alonzo. *He had better sleep with one eye open.*

Chapter 8

Five hours after the fight with Alonzo, I had successfully gotten the house in acceptable condition for Isaiah to return home. In the midst of my tantrum, I never once considered that my child would have to return to a house overwhelmed with bleach smell. So, in the middle of winter, I had every window and sliding glass door open to air out the house. Not a smart move on my part. However, the cold air did help me calm my anger and regain my composure. As for Alonzo's bleach-soaked and ripped clothing, I put them in trash bags and placed them in trashcans in the backyard. He was paid. Hell, he could go buy more clothes in an instant, or he could let his chocolate Candy Barr buy him a new wardrobe. I really didn't give a damn. I just cared about getting my home organized and cleaned before London brought Isaiah home.

It was almost ten o'clock at night. My baby had school the next day, and because I wanted to skin his father alive he couldn't come to his own home directly after school. This was yet another sign that it was time for Alonzo and me to part ways.

I called London and told her it was okay for her to bring Isaiah home. She said she was on her way. In the meantime, I wondered if Alonzo would be coming home or if he was too scared he might be greeted with a sharp blade when he entered the front door.

When I saw London's car lights in the driveway, I ran to the door and waited. "Hey, baby," I said to Isaiah as he approached, acting as if nothing were wrong. I had become such a professional actress when it came to disguising problems between me and his father. I never wanted Isaiah to be in the middle of our madness, so I never involved him.

"Hi, Mom," Isaiah said in a deep voice. I gave him a side hug as he entered the house.

"Hi, London," I said, giving her pouting eyes. "Thanks, girl. You know I love you, right?"

"I love you too. But I'd love you more if we were inside. It's cold out here," she said, shivering.

We walked in the house, and I closed the door behind us. Immediately, Isaiah grimaced and said, "Ew, Mom, why does it smell like bleach in here? It smells awful."

"Fix your face," I teased. "You're too handsome to be wearing such a scowl."

Everyone said that Isaiah was my twin. His eyes, lips, nose, and cheeks were all mine. Many described him as a really "pretty" boy because his features were so beautiful. But his coffee complexion and muscular physique were all Alonzo. He was a high school sports player, like Alonzo, but his sport of choice was basketball. As a sixteen-year-old, six-foot-tall, lightning-fast point guard, Isaiah had been told by his coaches that they saw a bright collegiate future with a scholarship for him. Because I hadn't had the college experience, I encouraged Isaiah, a straight-A student, to continue to do well in school. I supported his love of basketball, but my main focus was the academics.

"But why does it smell like that?" he said while squeezing his nostrils.

I hated lying to my child, but there was no way I was going to tell him what really had gone down earlier. "I accidentally spilled the entire bottle of bleach while trying to pour some in the bucket. I've been trying to air the house out. I thought it would be better by now."

"Well, it's not. It stinks."

"Sorry, baby." I looked down at my watch. It was time for Isaiah to prepare himself for school tomorrow. I needed to usher him out of the room so I could talk to London privately. "It's late, Isaiah. Please get your clothes out for tomorrow. You've got school."

"Okay, Mom. See you later, Cousin London. Thanks for picking me up from school."

"No problem. I'll see you later." She waved good-bye.

When Isaiah left the room, I gestured for London to come into the dining room where we could talk in private. As soon as she sat down, she asked, "What in the world is going on around here? I've been worried about you ever since you asked me to pick up Isaiah from school. What's wrong?"

In a whisper I said, "Alonzo strikes again."

"Huh?" She looked baffled.

"Oh, yes. My beloved husband strikes again."

"What do you mean?"

"Let's see. Where shall I begin? I went to class today, came home, and checked the mail. There was a pink envelope smelling like flowers addressed to Alonzo. It looked hella suspicious, so I opened it. In the envelope was a letter to Alonzo from a woman named Candice Barr."

London gasped. Her eyes widened. "No!"

"Yes!" I mimicked.

"What did the letter say?"

"Basically that she loves him, can't wait until our divorce is final so they can be together, that she promised to give him a better life than the one he's had with me, and thanked him for being her protector, provider, lover, and for paying her rent."

"Say *what?*" London said. "I mean, what the hell?"

"Girl, same Alonzo bullshit, just a different day. Ain't nothing new."

"What does this ho mean about divorce?"

"I don't know. As far as I knew, things were fine between us, but according to that letter, we are in the midst of a divorce."

"So, how do you know she's not lying? She could've made the whole thing up."

I gave London the side-eye, wondering if she really believed that the contents of that letter had just happened to fall out of the sky into my mailbox. Please. Nobody but Jesus could convince me that that woman was lying, and He hadn't done so yet.

I proceeded to tell London all about how the house had become overcome with the smell of bleach, the cutting of Alonzo clothes with the butcher knife, the altercation we had when he came home, and how I attempted to go Norman Bates on his ass just before he ran out of the house.

London's face was overcome with sadness. "Oh, Jaime. I'm so sorry you are going through this. Why didn't you tell me this earlier when we spoke? I would've come over then."

"There was no need to take you away from your job. I was okay. Hurt, yes. Taken aback, yes. Suicidal? No. Homicidal? Maybe, but not suicidal. I didn't want to get you all in an uproar over this."

"But, that's what friends and family are for. You shouldn't have been going through this alone. So, where is Alonzo now?"

"Don't know, don't care. I hope in hell."

"Jaime, y'all need to talk. Maybe consider getting marriage counseling or something."

"Black men don't do counseling. I don't see a psychologist in our future."

"But you've got to try," London pleaded. "At least for the sake of Isaiah. You and Alonzo have been through a lot and have overcome a lot. You just can't give up now. You're a fighter, Jaime. You can't let this other woman win."

"I don't have any fight left in me. I've been fighting for years for Alonzo to do right by me. He won't do it. I can't fight for this marriage by myself."

As London and I continued to talk, I felt a teardrop fall from my eye. I didn't want to cry over this. I no longer wanted to cry over Alonzo. I had been through too much with him and cried too many tears already. He didn't deserve my tears anymore.

"Aw, Jaime." London wrapped her arms around me. "It's gonna be okay. I promise you."

"I don't think so. Not this time."

"That's stinkin' thinkin', Jaime. You've got to trust in the Lord. Seek Him, pray about this."

My tears started flowing like a river. London had struck a nerve when she mentioned God. See, in the past, I could always call on Pastor Steele in times such as these, but now I didn't even have him, as he and Alonzo were two birds of a feather. Just thinking about how their behaviors mimicked one another made my disdain grow tenfold for each of them.

"I'm not sure how I'm going to handle this one. I've got no church home or pastor to lean on for spiritual guidance. I can't talk to my parents about this. I don't have the strength to pray. I don't know which way to turn."

"Well, you always have me and Riah if—"

"Shh," I whispered, stopping London mid-sentence. "Did you hear that?"

"No. What?" she voiced quietly.

"I think I just heard Isaiah's footsteps."

We sat quietly for a minute to listen for any other noises. There was nothing.

"Oh, my gosh. I hope Isaiah didn't hear us talking."

London said, "I thought we were pretty quiet, but you know kids these days. They hear and see things we don't think they do."

Worried that Isaiah may have overheard my conversation with London, she and I agreed to talk later. I told her that I was going to check on Isaiah to make sure he was prepared for school. I would try to examine his demeanor to determine if he had been eavesdropping on our discussion.

I sincerely hoped that Isaiah didn't know what was going on between Alonzo and me because I'd have been devastated. His knowing would mean I'd failed to protect him from all the ugly, dirty secrets about his father—secrets I never wanted him to know.

Chapter 9

The next morning, I could barely get out of bed to cook breakfast for Isaiah. I was physically tired and mentally drained. I hadn't gotten any sleep the night before, with my thoughts centered on the turmoil in my marriage. Alonzo hadn't come home, but that really didn't bother me. I actually thought that was for the best. I wasn't as concerned about Alonzo as I was at the possibility of Isaiah eavesdropping as I'd opened up to London about the problems involving Alonzo and me.

After London's departure, I briefly talked to Isaiah, who didn't seem any different. Then, while he ate breakfast, I examined his behavior as we chatted, but I didn't observe any changes. He even seemed excited about the basketball game he had after school. I thought I knew my son pretty well, and I was almost certain that he hadn't heard the conversation between London and me.

Once Isaiah left for the morning, I headed back to bed. I was going to skip my digital photography class because I was too exhausted to focus on anything but sleeping.

The moment I closed my eyes, the doorbell rang. Perplexed as to who would be at my door so early in the morning, I peeped out the bedroom window to see if I saw a recognizable car. I did. It was my dad's car. *What in the world?* I put on my bathrobe, slid my feet into my slippers, and rushed to the door.

I opened the door, squinting to block out the bright sunlight. "Ma? Dad? I didn't know y'all were coming over."

Walking directly past me, my father said, "Are you okay, Jaime?"

I closed the door behind them. "Yes, Dad. Why?"

"What's going on with you and Alonzo?" my dad asked, getting straight to the point.

I was caught off guard. I had no idea my parents were aware of the turbulence in my home. I didn't even want them to know. Now they were here, standing in my living room, questioning me about something that I wanted to keep hidden.

"What . . . what do you mean?" I asked nervously.

My mother spoke. "Jaime, we know you and Alonzo are going through some problems. We know there was a big argument about a woman. We know bleach was used, and we know he wasn't here last night. We also know there was some talk about divorce. What we don't know are the details and whether you're all right."

"Oh, my. Who told you all of that?" I was baffled.

My dad spoke. "Isaiah. He called us last night around midnight, whispering on the phone. Upset. Telling us how much he hates his dad."

"Oh, no. He heard us?" I was immediately horrified.

"What do you mean?" Mom asked.

"Last night, London and I were in the dining room talking about what happened between Alonzo and me. We thought we were whispering. Then I heard foot-steps. We stopped talking, thinking it was Isaiah. But later, when I talked to him, he didn't act as if anything was wrong, so I assumed I was just hearing things."

"No, honey. You weren't hearing things," Dad chimed in. "That boy heard everything y'all said. He said after he listened to y'all, he called Alonzo. Alonzo told him he was out riding around, clearing his thoughts, and said that he would be home later. When Isaiah questioned him about what happened between the two of you, Alonzo's responses were vague. He didn't give Isaiah any straight answers, which made him angry. He then called us and said he knows all about his dad cheating on his mom with some woman, and that you two were getting a divorce, and he hates how his dad mistreats his mom."

I burst into tears. "Never in a million years did I ever want my child to be subjected to this chaos. He doesn't deserve this. I feel so bad."

"Jaime," my mother said, putting her arm around me. "Don't blame yourself for all of this. You didn't know Isaiah was listening. You also didn't know he called Alonzo or what Alonzo was going to say. You had no control over that."

"But, Mom, I bleached all of Alonzo's clothes and shoes and Isaiah had to come home to the house smelling like that. That's so not fair to him."

"Jaime, let's back up for a minute," Dad requested. "Please tell us what happened from the beginning. We've only gotten bits and pieces of this story. What happened?"

I shook my head in disbelief. I so didn't want to get into this with my parents. "Dad, you know I don't like draggin' y'all into my marital issues."

"You're not draggin' us into this. Your son called us last night at midnight, saddened, expressing his disdain for his dad. When Isaiah made that call, he made us a part of it. When you're hurt or our grandson is hurting, we all hurt. So don't look at it as though you've put us in the middle," Dad stated firmly. I could tell from his tone that he was not leaving without answers.

"All right," I groaned. "Long story short. Yesterday after class, I came home and found a suspicious envelope in the mail addressed to Alonzo. The letter inside was from a woman named Candice Barr that said she's in love with Alonzo, and that she can't wait for our divorce to be final. She promised to treat him better than I do, and mentioned how he's been a great protector, lover, yada, yada, yada." My stomach ached as I relived the contents of that heart-wrenching letter over again. Each time I retold the story or even thought about it, I felt cramping pains in my stomach. When I attempted to eat, I would feel burning sensations in my stomach that would force me to push my plate away. This situation with Alonzo was taking its toll on me emotionally and physically.

My father's face bore an irritated expression. "So, what did Alonzo have to say about all of this?"

"He says he only knows this woman as an associate from working in DC. He claims she's lying, making it all up, and that he's being framed." I grabbed my belly again, as I felt constipation-like pains in my stomach.

My mother noticed. "Jaime, why are you holding your stomach?"

"It hurts. Sometimes I feel like I'm cramping, and other times it burns when I eat. I've been feeling like this since all this turmoil with Alonzo."

Mom looked at me with worry. "Jaime, I love you, and I am deeply sorry that you are going through this with Alonzo. I'm praying to God that what he says is true about this women being a liar. Have you two talked?"

"The last time we talked, it wasn't pretty. I destroyed all his clothes and shoes and attempted to attack him with a butcher knife. So, no; technically, we haven't talked. We've argued, but not talked."

"Butcher knife, Jaime? Now, you know better," Dad said.

"I know. I know."

"Well, listen," Dad said, "your mother and I have always tried to allow you to make your own decisions. So we're not going to tell you what to do. I don't like what's going on one bit. Not a bit. And I know what I'd like to do to Alonzo right now, but I am going to respect you as an adult and trust that you will do what's best for you and my grandson. With that said, you know you weren't raised in a violent home, and Isaiah shouldn't be subjected to that either. So, if you and Alonzo don't think you can talk this out like level-headed adults, then you may need to consider going your separate ways until you can. Domestic violence is not the answer to this. Reactions made in the heat of the moment can land you in jail, baby, and your son needs his mother."

"Dad, I'm sorry. I just wasn't thinking clearly. I know better."

"Don't apologize to us," he said. "You're hurting. You're angry. I understand that. I just want to make you aware that there are other options. Hell, if you need to come and stay with your mother and me, you know our door is always open."

"Thanks, Dad."

"Now, Jaime," Mom interjected, "ever since we've been here, you've been having those pains. I'm concerned about you. I can only imagine the stress you're under. I want you to consider going to the doctor. Just to be on the safe side. Stomach cramping and burning may be stress related, but I want you to get a professional opinion just in case."

"Okay, Mom. I will."

My parents and I talked a little more in depth about the fight with Alonzo and how I should handle it. I could tell my dad wanted me to leave. Words like "you don't have to put up with this" and "nobody deserves to live like this" kept flying from his mouth. I couldn't say I was surprised. I was his only child, his baby girl. He didn't take pleasure in seeing my anguish. My mom, on the other hand, hated to see marriages dissolve. Before encouraging me to give up on Alonzo, she'd suggest counseling and prayer.

"Mom and Dad, I thank y'all for coming over. I really needed this talk. I feel better. I think before I make any rash decisions, I will sit down and have a heart-to-heart with Alonzo. I'm just not ready yet."

"Remember to talk with your mouth, young lady," Dad ordered, "not with your hands or weapons or household cleaning products."

Inwardly I chuckled.

"Since you're dealing with a lot right now, let Isaiah spend the weekend with us," Mom suggested. "It's Friday. He has a game after school today. We can go to his game, and then take him home with us after. I think you and Alonzo need some alone time."

"That's fine, Mom, but I really need to talk to him. I need to find out how he's feeling about what he overheard. My heart is breaking for him right now."

"Agreed. We'll bring him home after the game to pack a bag for the weekend, and you can talk to him then."

"Good. Thanks. I appreciate you two." I hugged both of them tightly.

"We love you, Jaime. I know you're going through a rough time right now, but I want you to remember to pray. God is listening."

I gave a fake smile. I appreciated my mother's comforting wording, but any mention of church, God, or the Bible was such a sore spot for me. It just made me loathe Pastor Steele even more. I despised him for being an oversexed freak, thus not being able to placate me during one of the toughest times of my life.

Right after my parents left, the pain in my abdomen was persistent, and I felt the urgent need to defecate. I ran to the bathroom, fearful that I wasn't going to make it before my bowels exploded. I hurriedly ripped off my bathrobe, pulled down my pajama pants, and plopped onto the toilet. Instantly, everything in my small intestines was released. I had diarrhea.

"Whew, that was close," I softly said to myself. "I almost didn't make it."

I thought my mom was right. My body was beginning to succumb to all the physical and mental pressure.

Chapter 10

Alonzo

"What the hell is your problem, Alonzo?" Candice questioned as I brushed passed her and entered her apartment.

I was mad as hell at her for that letter-writing stunt, and I was about to dig in that ass about it. "I can't fucking believe you," I roared. "What in the world would possess you to send that letter to my house? Have you lost your mind?"

I had just arrived at Candice's apartment. Usually, when I laid eyes upon her flawless cinnamon skin and big brown eyes, I'd want to immediately take her to the bedroom and sex her until I no longer had strength left in my body. But today was different. The last two days had been a total nightmare for me. I hadn't been at home. I hadn't been to work. I'd had to go shopping for clothing and toiletries, and I was sleeping in a hotel room. I couldn't believe that I, a U.S. Department of Justice attorney, had allowed myself to get caught up in such a mess. And, to top it off, I'd had the uncomfortable experience of having to explain to my son why he had overheard his mother talking to London about my having an affair with another woman. He asked me if I was cheating on his mother. He questioned me about why I made his mother cry. He wanted to know if his mother and I were divorcing. He even said,

"If you don't love Mommy anymore, then maybe you shouldn't come back home." I was crushed. I had made many mistakes in my lifetime, but none bothered me more than answering my cell phone and hearing my son's voice on the other end, pleading with me to make things right with his mother or stay away forever.

I took a couple of days trying to clear my head before returning home, and I wanted to give Jaime some space and time to cool off. She and I needed to have a heart-to-heart, but before I addressed her, I felt it was more urgent to confront Candice and give her a piece of my mind.

"No, I haven't lost my mind. Why would you assume that?" she asked with a straight face.

"Are you kidding me? You've got to be kidding me. You send a letter with red lip prints on it, sprayed with perfume, to my house, and you don't think my wife would see that shit?"

"But she isn't supposed to be there. Aren't you two separated? Almost divorced?"

"Hell, no!" I retorted. "Where did you get that from?"

"From you."

I was totally confused. I had never told this woman I was leaving my wife. She stood there, looking at my face, telling me I told her that. She must have been absolutely crazy. "What would lead you to believe that? Come on. I've never said that to you."

"Well, let's see. You spend late nights with me. You have sex with me. You pay my bills. And how often have you told me you're unhappy at home? Duh! Why wouldn't I believe you were in the process of leaving your wife?"

"You're delusional," I hollered. "Yes, my wife and I have had issues, but I never, ever told you we were separated and heading for divorce. Never! Yes, we've had some late-night rendezvous, messed around, had some fun, but that's all it was for me. Fun! I wasn't planning to have a future with you. And I've only paid one of your bills. Only one, and that was your rent when you cried about not having the money and were scared you'd get an eviction notice. I thought of you as a friend. I didn't want to see your belongings set out on the streets. So, yes, I helped. But you made it seem like it was a regular occurrence."

"Stop yelling at me like I'm the enemy. I'm not. And I'm definitely not delusional. You have led me to believe time and time again that you and I were heading toward something more. If I was just a one-night stand, then it would've stopped after the first time we had sex in your office. But it continued. Why the cute little e-mails telling me 'Good morning' or 'Have a nice day' if there was nothing more?"

I was getting so frustrated. I almost wanted to put my hands around her neck. "Oh, my gosh! That was some cordial shit I was doing after having sex with you, so you wouldn't feel like I was just sexing you and not calling you the next day. It only went on for as long as it did because, well, I enjoyed the freaky shit you did to me."

"Fuck you, Alonzo! Fuck you! I hate you!" she yelled, grabbing a pillow from her sofa and hurling it at my head.

"Stop throwing shit. Be an adult, for goodness' sake. You brought this on yourself. Things were cool just the way they were, but then you decided to write that letter, no doubt trying to mess up my home life."

"That's not true," she defended herself. "I didn't know your wife lived there."

"That's bull! And you know it. But, hey, it was good while it lasted. I'm not going to argue with you about this anymore. Since you just yelled how much you hate me, then it shouldn't be hard for you not to contact me again. Don't call me. Don't e-mail me. And please don't send any more letters to my damn house. I'm not leaving my wife, and I'm not ever going to be with you. Got it? Good."

Candy got a deranged look in her eyes. It was a look similar to the one Jaime gave right before she charged toward me with that knife. I needed to start making my way to the door because I didn't want this to be a real-life *Fatal Attraction* moment.

"What-the-fuck-ever." Candy laughed. "You been sniffing behind my ass for the past nine months, and now you want to declare that it's over. You're a joke."

"It's not a joke. This adulterous relationship was wrong on so many levels, and it never should've started. Now that my wife is all in an uproar. My son knows and is devastated, no doubt looking at me differently as a man. It's all because you decided to announce to my family via the U.S. Postal Service that we were having an affair. This can't and won't continue. So you can think it's a joke all you want, but I'm telling you I'm finished—we're finished."

"So, now you have a conscience?" Again she expressed amusement. "Now you care about your son? Funny how every time you tapped my booty, he didn't seem to cross your mind. Now all of a sudden you care? Like I said, you're a joke."

Candy's comment stung a little. "I've always cared about my son. And that's all I'm going to say about that because I don't have to explain nothin' to you about him. All you need to know is that this friendship, or whatever you want to call it, is over. Forget you know me, as I will forget all about you." I waited a couple of seconds to hear her response, but there was none. I assumed she had gotten the message. Now it was time for me to go. "It's been real. Now, I gotta go." I turned to walk away, and headed toward the apartment door.

As I placed my hand on the doorknob, I heard Candy scream, "*No, Alonzo.* Don't leave." I turned around to see her rushing toward me. Before I could react, she had dropped to her knees, wrapped her arms around my legs, and begun wailing like a baby. "I'm so sorry, Alonzo. I love you. Please forgive me. I'll do anything to make it right. Just don't go. *Don't go.*"

I looked down at her and shook my head. I couldn't believe that this chick was actually hugging my thighs and crying like somebody had died.

"Candy, please let my legs go," I firmly said. "I'm leaving now. It was not my intent to hurt you, but you overstepped your boundaries when you sent that note to my house. I can no longer have any dealings with you. I just can't." I tried to find a sympathetic bone in my body, but simply didn't have one. Candy knew exactly what she was doing when she dropped that envelope in the mail. She knew she would wreak havoc in my life. For somebody who claimed that she loved me, she sure had a distorted way of showing it.

"I'm so *sorry.* I really am. I didn't mean to hurt you or your son. I didn't. Please believe me."

Candy wasn't getting it. No amount of pleas would get me to change my mind. There would be no second chances. Ever.

I forcibly pried her arms from around my legs.

"Stop it, Alonzo! Stop it!" she bellowed as she attempted to stop me from peeling her arms from around my kneecaps.

"Get off me, Candy, now! I'm trying to leave, and you're keeping me here against my will. That's against the law. Now, if I have to call the police, I will. The choice is yours." With my cell phone in hand, I dialed nine and one, and was all set to dial the last digit until she released her grip.

"Just go, you bastard! Get out!" she screamed at the top of her lungs.

Without a second thought, I ran out of there like a bat out of hell. The scene at Candy's apartment was more dramatic than I'd ever expected. I was glad to finally be free and out of her presence. Hopefully, she got the message loud and clear that I was done with her. Fooling around with her was a huge mistake—one I'd never make again.

Driving back to the hotel, I felt a little relief knowing that I had gotten the talk with Candy out of the way. Now it was time to go home to face Jaime. I planned to spend one more night at the hotel, but by tomorrow morning I'd be going back to my home, hopefully making amends with my wife, saving my marriage, and regaining the respect I'd lost from my son.

Chapter 11

Jaime

Early Saturday morning, London and Riah called to say they were coming to take me out to lunch. They wanted to get me out of the house for some fresh air and a good meal. After the problems I had been having with my stomach, I had no desire to eat, but I did look forward to being in the company of friends. I was kind of depressed after speaking with Isaiah.

After Isaiah's game, my parents had brought him home to pack a bag for the weekend. We sat in his room, just the two of us, and discussed what he'd overheard and his feelings about the situation.

"Isaiah, Grandpop told me that you called him last night around midnight, upset about the conversation you overheard between London and me. Is that true?"

Isaiah looked down toward the floor. I could tell he didn't want to talk about what was going on with his dad and me, but I needed to hear his thoughts.

"Look at me, Isaiah," I said, lifting his head. "Tell me what happened."

"Well, I came down to the kitchen for a glass of water and I thought I heard you crying. So I stopped to listen. That's when I heard you say that Dad was cheating with some lady and that you two were going to divorce and stuff."

"Oh, baby. I am so sorry you had to find out that way. I never wanted you to know any of this."

"Why? I'm not a baby, Mom. I have a right to know."

"True, you're not a baby, Isaiah, but I don't think you should be involved in things that are going on between your dad and me. Your only concerns should be school, basketball, and video games."

"So, are you two getting a divorce?"

"I don't know, Isaiah. We have not talked about that yet."

"I called him, and I told him that if he doesn't make things right with you then to never come back home."

"Are you angry with him?"

"Yeah. How could he treat you like this? You're, like, the best mom in the world, and all you do is think about us."

"I don't have all the answers right now, but I want you to know that no matter what happens between us, none of this is your fault. And we both still love you very much."

"Hmph. Well, Dad can't love us if he's out with other women."

"Don't say that, Isaiah. Your dad loves you. Believe me when I say this has nothing to do with you. Nothing. His love for you will never change."

"Well . . . well . . . I look at him differently now. I'm not sure I respect him as much. I mean, how can he give me all these speeches on how to treat young girls and how to be a respectable young boy when he's not doing those things himself?"

Isaiah had a point, and damn near left me speechless. I was tired as hell of trying to defend Alonzo and his actions to our son. He had left me in one heck of a predicament. He was the one rolling around in bed with tramp after tramp, but I was the one left at home trying to defend his actions to our sixteen-year-old son. This was so unfair.

Isaiah and I talked for about forty-five minutes while my parents waited patiently for us to finish. We agreed to talk further once he returned home on Sunday. I wasn't sure how much comfort I provided him, so I asked my father if he could spend some quality time with Isaiah to help talk him through this situation. My father agreed.

Once they left, I felt alone and empty. There I was, all alone, left with nothing but my thoughts. I needed an escape, so I took two Benadryl tablets to help me fall asleep.

When I got the call from London and Riah the next morning, I was elated. Although I knew it was going to take every ounce of strength I had to get showered and dressed, I welcomed the outing with London and Riah. I needed to get out, be with friends.

London, Riah, and I went to a small café in Old Town Alexandria for lunch. This restaurant was one of our favorite mom-and-pop restaurants. Their deli sandwiches and cheesecake were absolutely delicious. But I only watched as London ordered a corned beef sandwich on rye, and Riah ordered a roasted turkey and Swiss sandwich. I ordered chicken noodle soup.

"Come on, Jaime. You've got to eat more than soup," Riah demanded.

"I can't really eat anything heavy. Whenever I eat, my stomach burns. The only things that don't seem to irritate my stomach are soup, bread, and other bland foods. As much as I want one of those sandwiches, I just can't eat it."

"When did this start?" London queried.

"Take a wild guess."

"Right when this Alonzo stuff started, right?" Riah said.

"You got it. I could've been having problems before, but just didn't notice it."

"Have you considered seeing a doctor?"

"Yeah. My mom suggested the same thing. I just haven't had time to see straight."

"Your health is important. Don't ignore this." London had that same look of concern that my mother had had in her eyes.

"I won't."

The girls and I made small talk until the waiter brought our food. Once our meals arrived, Riah wasted no time offering her opinion on my marital woes in between bites of her sandwich. "Jaime, you know I love you. I've been your friend for twenty years, so please don't be offended by anything that I'm going to say."

"Okay. I'm listening."

"Alonzo said that what the whore said in her letter wasn't true, right?"

"Right."

"Well, have you called the bitch or contacted her in some way?" Riah was getting steamed.

"No, Riah. I'm not calling that woman. I am so sick and tired of doing that. Do you know how many times I've called women, sent e-mails, threatened them, told them to leave my man alone, yada, yada, yada? I'm too old for that stuff now, and it doesn't make a damn bit of difference 'cause if he still wants to mess with this woman, he will. Besides, I don't have the energy to fight these women for Alonzo anymore."

"I agree," London stated. "Alonzo is her problem. Not that other woman."

"Y'all crazy. If it were me, I'd be cutting Everett and the tramp. Hell, he'd feel the wrath because he knew better, and I'd slice and dice her ass because the bitch knew he was married. When it comes to cheating, nobody gets a pass. Nobody."

I just smiled at Riah because she was dead serious. When it came to her relationship, she was always no-nonsense about infidelity and always vowed that she would cut both her husband and the other woman into little pieces.

"I was already hurt by the words in her letter. I really don't want to talk to her. I've learned that calling the other woman only hurts you more. They can and will say things to make your heart ache."

"You ain't lying," London said. "They get pleasure out of saying things like 'your husband likes to toss my salad' or 'he told me he was only with you because of the child.' Y'all know that hurtful mess they say because deep down inside they have low self-esteem. Hell, if they could get their own man, they wouldn't be laid up with somebody else's husband."

"Amen to that." Riah gave London a high-five. "I can't stand those skanky whores. I can't. But, enough about that beyotch. What are you going to do about Alonzo?"

I hunched my shoulders. "I have no idea."

"What are your feelings now?" London asked. "When we talked a couple days ago, you seemed adamant about the marriage being over. Do you still feel that way?"

I looked down at my bowl of uneaten soup. I was trying to gather my thoughts into words. "I don't know. I mean, in a perfect world, I would love for my marriage to overcome this and for Alonzo and me to live happily ever after. But so much has happened with us, and I just don't ever see it getting better. His track record for infidelity is off the charts. Obviously, he has no respect for me, our son, or our union. I don't have any hope for us as a couple anymore. I just don't." I felt tears forming in my eyes as the reality of my marriage hit me with those words.

"Jaime, you've got to try counseling," London pleaded. "I don't want you to give up. Not yet, especially since you haven't really talked to Alonzo about this. You have no idea where his head is right now. He may be just as devastated by this as you."

I smirked. "Yeah, right. He hasn't been home for the past two days. Undoubtedly, he's laid up with his jump-off."

Riah's face wore a look of disapproval. "London, I understand you're all about family preservation, but how can we as her friends ask her to endure the mess Alonzo continues to put her through? He's been cheating on her for years. *Years.* When does this infidelity crap stop? And when does she say enough is enough? I'm tired of seeing her go through this. I really am. She doesn't deserve it, so if she wants to kick that Negro to the curb, I'm all for it." Riah held up the peace sign.

"We'll just have to agree to disagree," London yelped. "I'm not telling her to stay in a relationship where she is going to be continually emotionally abused. I'd never suggest that. But, in this instance, she hasn't even sat down and talked with her husband. How can she make any decisions if she hasn't talked with her spouse? That makes no sense."

Riah and London's exchange was becoming a bit heated. They were talking as if I weren't even sitting there.

"What is there to talk about?" Riah asked. "What more does she need? We all know Alonzo doesn't have a faithful bone in his body. He's a good provider for his family, but he sucks at everything else. When all the stuff went down at church, he offered the least amount of support to Jaime. His work hours are often late 'cause his job is so much more important than his family. When was the last time they took a family vacation? Alonzo is a poor excuse for a husband, and I know Jaime can do better."

London just rolled her eyes at Riah. Because London didn't like scenes, I was sure that's why she didn't continue to go back and forth with Riah. My guess was that this conversation between the two of them wasn't done.

"My dear cousin, and my dear friend, I know y'all are looking out for me, but don't allow my situation to cause you two to bicker. It's so not worth it. Now, Riah, I feel you. Alonzo could be a better husband in many areas. And, in my heart, I want to leave him, but I can't."

Riah glared at me. "Why is that?"

"Because I can't. I depend on him for everything. I have no job, no income, and without him, I'd have nothing."

"That's B.S., Jaime, and you know it. You could always go back to your parents' house to live, and you can find a job."

"But I don't want to go back to my parents' house. I want to live in my house. I want to be surrounded by the things I've become accustomed to."

"Then take his ass to divorce court and get alimony."

"That's an idea," I agreed. "But I'm not at that point yet. In my mind, I've checked out of the marriage. Alonzo has hurt me for the last time. Unless he can show me he's a changed man, we're married in name only. I plan to save up my money, possibly go job hunting, and do whatever I can to make it on my own, because I'm not expecting our marriage to last."

I looked over at London, who didn't seem happy about my decision. "London, don't be mad at me. I've got to protect my heart. I'm through being the good wife. I don't have the strength to do it anymore. However, I will do as you suggested and have a sit-down talk with Alonzo. Maybe after talking to him, my outlook will change. I doubt it, but at least I can give it a try."

"I'm not angry with you at all, Jaime," London said. "I just don't want you to make hasty decisions. Also, keep Isaiah in mind and what's best for him. But, if in your heart you really want to leave Alonzo, please don't let dependency keep you in this marriage. As long as you have our support, you can and will survive."

"I know that's right." Riah finally agreed with something London said.

The lunch date with my friends was a good outing. Although the conversation was mainly about my issues with Alonzo, it felt good to be out. After lunch, I found myself going back and forth between London's opinion and Riah's opinion. Both of them had made valid points; however, I really didn't know what I was going to do. If there was a chance I could make my marriage work, I would have loved to do so, but I doubted it. And it was that constant doubt that made me throw my hands up in defeat and just let Alonzo go.

I didn't have my mind made up, but I felt my heart leaning more toward washing my hands of marriage.

Chapter 12

After lunch with the girls, I found myself tearing up the two lanes on George Washington Parkway, heading home. I felt my stomach about to implode again. Initially, I felt constipated. Now, I felt like I could go any second. These ongoing stomach issues were beginning to concern me. I definitely needed to make an appointment with a physician as soon as possible.

When I pulled into my driveway, I noticed that Alonzo's car was there. "Shoot! I am not in the mood for him today." I didn't know what finally made him decide to come home, but I was not happy with him being here. I wasn't ready to lay eyes upon him yet. I was still extremely angry with him, and I wanted to honor my father's wishes and not resort to domestic violence when talking to him.

I jumped out of my car and ran to the door. The need to use the bathroom was critical, or else I'd be soaked in feces, smelling like a horse stable. As I approached the door, it opened. Alonzo greeted me at the door. "Hi, Jaime."

"What are you doing here?" I snapped.

"I live here," he replied calmly. "And I wanna talk."

"Not right now. I gotta go to the bathroom."

I ripped my coat off and threw it on the living room chair. I started running up the stairs, headed toward the bathroom in the master bedroom, unbuttoning my pants as I climbed the stairs. When I reached the bathroom, I snatched down my pants and sat. Immediately, my soup was released.

As soon as I moved my bowels, I always felt better. The stomach burning and the diarrhea episodes were the main reasons I had no desire to eat.

Upon leaving the bathroom, I was startled by Alonzo, who was sitting on the bed, waiting for me. I looked at him, but didn't say a word.

"Jaime, can we talk?" he asked.

With my back to him, digging in the closet and trying to find a comfortable outfit to throw on, I asked, "About?"

"About us. About what happened recently. About everything."

Honestly, I didn't feel like talking to Alonzo, but everybody kept urging me to talk to him, talk things through, communicate, get things out in the open, so I figured I'd agree. Besides, Isaiah wasn't home, so it was a good time to speak freely without having to worry about him overhearing anything.

"Listen, I'm willing to talk, but I don't want to hear your lies, Alonzo. I'm tired of lies. We're too old for this mess. So, if you can't come correct, don't come at all."

"I promise I will be one hundred percent truthful with you. I swear."

I rolled my eyes. To me, he was already lying. This Negro didn't have a truthful bone in his body. "Whatever, Alonzo. Say what you gotta say."

I sat Indian style on the opposite side of the bed, facing Alonzo. I placed a pillow in my lap, looked him directly in his eyes, and prepared myself to listen to the load of bull he was about to spew.

"Jaime, first let me start by saying how much I love you. You have been by my side through thick and thin. I know I can count on you to be in my corner when no one else is there. I appreciate you for being a loving, caring, supportive wife and mother. I'm so sorry I have not lived up to your expectations as a husband."

Alonzo's comments were nice, but my heart was too cold at this point to be moved by his statements.

"Now, I promised you that I was going to be honest with you, so I want to warn you that you are not gonna like everything I'm about to say. But I'm comin' clean about everything regarding this Candice situation."

Instantly, my stomach ached. Women always claim they want to know the whole truth and nothing but the truth. But do we really? I wasn't so sure I was prepared for what he was about to say.

Alonzo took a deep breath. I could tell he was uncomfortable. "Nine months ago, I met Candice. She works for the U.S. Department of Housing and Urban Development in DC. You may know it as HUD. Anyway, a legal issue came up within her department, so they contacted the Justice Department. My team of lawyers was assigned to the case. Candice came over to our building with her team, which consisted of three people, she being the lead. On my team, I was the leader for this particular case. Once our teams met, we had a two-hour meeting. No issues were resolved. At the end of that meeting, Candice and I exchanged business cards and agreed to meet again to discuss the legal matters. The next time we met, we had a working lunch. The time after that, we had a working dinner. The third time was at my office, where . . . where . . ."

Alonzo stopped talking and my heart started racing. I knew where this was headed. I was torn. I wanted to know more, but really I didn't.

"You had sex with her in your office, right?"

With his head hung low, he confirmed it. "Yeah. I did. I'm so sorry."

I knew I'd said I wasn't going to shed any more tears over Alonzo, but I couldn't help it. I loved him, and no matter how many times he'd cheated, it still hurt. The fact that he sat there admitting it to me was like driving a switchblade into my heart. It damaged my soul.

"Jaime, I'm so sorry. I really am. I have no excuses for my behavior except that I'm a selfish bastard. And you're right when you said I think about no one but myself."

"So, all those times you had to work late on such an important case, you were sexing Miss Candy Barr, huh? Not giving a damn about how it would make me or Isaiah feel."

"Oftentimes, I really am working, that's true. However, there have been times when I was with her."

I threw the pillow at him. "You fuckin' make me sick. I wish I had never married your ass. You've put me through more hell than any enemy could've ever done. For someone who claims to love me, you've hurt me more than anyone else in this world. You don't love me. You can't love me."

"Jaime, you have every right to be upset with me. I've been horrible to you over the years. I know you don't trust me and may have a hard time forgiving me for this, but I want your forgiveness. I want to make this work. I want to change. I want my family more than anything in this world. I want to be a better husband and father. I want to help you to trust me again. I promise I'll work really hard at becoming a better man."

Alonzo's plea for forgiveness seemed sincere, and, I had to admit, I'd never seen this side of him in the past when caught up in his web of lies. But these were words coming from Alonzo. His words held no merit.

"So, we're not getting a divorce like the letter said?" I questioned.

"Hell no. I never told her that. I even went to her apartment and told her to stay out of my life. For the past couple of days, I've been staying in a hotel, contemplating if I wanted to jeopardize my career, law license, and my freedom for killing her for what she did to me. I never led her to believe we were going to be together. She's delusional, and I told her that. Candice is no longer a part of my life, personally or professionally. I want nothing more to do with her ever again. You and Isaiah are my focus. That's all I care about right now."

"Don't go blaming all this on her. Yes, she may be crazy, but you decided to lie down with her. Maybe, had you not stepped outside your marriage, you wouldn't have to deal with a delusional-ass broad like Candy."

"No argument here," Alonzo agreed. He reached across the bed and placed his hand on top of mine. "Jaime, for the rest of my days on earth, I am going to make this up to you. You have been my rock, my backbone, and I'm so grateful to you for raising our son alone, putting your dreams aside, allowing me to pursue mine, and for putting up with my bullshit. I mean, the list is endless. I love you, and I apologize for everything."

Still miffed at Alonzo, I said, "Your words hold no weight with me. I don't trust you. Actions speak louder than words. Your actions will be the true testament, but what you say out of your mouth has no value with me."

"I understand. I thank you for giving me a chance to prove myself. I guarantee I will make this up to you and Isaiah. I promise."

Alonzo walked over to the side of the bed where I was sitting. "May I give you a hug?"

"Why?"

"I just wanna wrap my arms around you and tell you I love you."

"I don't care," I responded nonchalantly.

He reached down, gently hugged me, kissed my cheek, and softly said, "I love you." He then left the room. I'd have been lying if I said that I didn't appreciate Alonzo vowing to be a better man and wanting to make an attempt to make things better between us. But I just didn't buy it. I had been through too much with him for so many years. What made this time so different? Why the need to change now? I wasn't fully buying this "changed man" speech.

My heart was still covered with bitterness. If Alonzo thought all was forgiven and life would resume as normal, he was sadly mistaken.

Chapter 13

Two weeks after my conversation with Alonzo, I still woke up every morning feeling like crap. Nothing had changed for me. If anything, things were worse. I had become a complete introvert. I had neither liveliness nor a desire to do anything except lie in bed and watch television. My classmate, Mario, had reached out to me a couple of times to inquire why I hadn't shown up for our digital photography class. I'd told him that I was going through some things that would impact my ability to concentrate in class.

I was overcome with feelings of sadness, hopelessness, and emptiness. I felt mentally and physically fatigued. I never wanted to open the curtains or the blinds in the house as I wanted it to remain dark at all times. It helped me to sleep better—whenever I wasn't dealing with insomnia. The persistent aches and pains in my stomach had not ceased. I was noticeably starting to lose weight, but I still had not made an appointment to see a doctor because I couldn't find the energy to make the call.

Alonzo had been true to his word so far in trying to prove to me that he wanted to save our marriage. He had flowers delivered to the house; he bought a new diamond necklace for me, and sent cards just to say "I love you." When at work, he called throughout the day to check on me, he kept me abreast of his schedule, and he would call to let me know his whereabouts. He had been staying home more often, even prepared a few meals. Even with his nice gestures, I still found myself extremely paranoid every time he left the house. When he said, "I'm going to the gym to work out," immediately I thought it was a lie. Or when he said, "I'm going to the mall," my thoughts: *lie*. Or, "I'm going to get an oil change." *Lie*. Nothing he said was the truth. It didn't matter if he said the sun was shining or it was snowing or there were clouds in the sky or his last name was Clarke—all of it was a lie.

I could see that Alonzo was making the attempt at change, but I couldn't allow myself to fall into his trap again. It had only been a couple of weeks. Any man could be on his best behavior for a few weeks. And I wasn't buying what he was selling—not just yet. He had a lot more proving to do to me.

My phone had been ringing nonstop since I opened my eyes. I had no desire to talk to anyone, but I knew that if I didn't answer the phone, my friends and family might send the police over to my house. When I looked at the caller ID and saw Riah's number, I decided to take the call.

"Hi, Riah," I answered.

"Jamie Clarke," she snapped. "I've been calling you for three days. Why have you not been returning my calls?"

"Forgive me. I just haven't been feeling up to talkin' to anybody."

"Oh, *baby*. What's wrong?" Riah asked compassionately.

"I can't explain it. I just feel like I'm in a dark place right now. I have no energy to do anything. I have no desire to do anything. I have no appetite, and I just feel sad—downright sad."

"It's understandable. You've gone through a lot already this year. Sounds like you're a little depressed. Do you want me to come over after I leave work? Or would you like to try to go out today to do something to pamper yourself, like a manicure or pedicure?"

"Naw, that's okay," I politely declined. "I may take you up on that offer later though."

"Well, if I call you later, will you answer? I'd like to check back with you this evening."

"Yeah, I'll pick up."

"All right. I'll call you later. I love you, and I'm praying for you."

"Love you too."

As soon as I hung up the phone with Riah, I rolled over and closed my eyes. I just wanted to sleep, as that was my escape from life, from pain, from sadness.

A few hours later, Isaiah arrived home from school. He walked into my bedroom and called out for me. "Ma," he said softly.

"Huh?" I responded with my face buried in my pillow.

"I'll come back when you're awake." He turned to walk away.

"No, Isaiah. Come back. I'm up. What's wrong?" I sat up quickly in bed to give Isaiah my attention. Something was wrong. I could tell by the sullen look on his face. He and Alonzo's relationship had been estranged even with Alonzo trying to make amends. Isaiah had remained noticeably distant from him these past couple of weeks. Alonzo definitely needed more than flowers, cards, jewelry, and dinner to earn back the respect of his son.

"Well, um, well . . . I got my report card today," he said, handing it to me with his head down, eyes glued to the floor.

I unfolded the report card, which Isaiah had folded into four squares. When I scanned the grades, I was stunned to see that they had dropped tremendously. "Isaiah, your grades look horrible!"

He didn't speak. He just stood in the middle of my bedroom floor with a gloomy expression.

"You've got a C in English and Ds in math and history. Last quarter, you had all As. How did your grades drop so drastically in one quarter?"

He hunched his shoulders, but still didn't speak.

Firmly, I said, "Isaiah Clarke, you better open your mouth now, and stop hunching your shoulders at me. Now, tell me, how does an above-average, straight-A student go to performing below average?"

"I don't know, Ma. I guess I wasn't as focused as I should've been last quarter. I'll try harder this quarter."

"Oh, no, no, no, buddy. Don't think you're gettin' off that easy with that next quarter speech. This is unlike you. I need an explanation as to why this has happened. My child doesn't get Cs and Ds—ever. So why now?"

"I missed turning in a few assignments and didn't do well on some test and quizzes. I haven't been studying like I should."

"Well, I hope you know that this puts you in jeopardy with the basketball team. Your coach is serious about academic success, and, right now, you're barely displaying it. Now, since you have fallen short on completing assignments and studying, I want you to spend some time in your room to think about a plan of action to ensure that you won't bring home these type of grades next quarter. And later, when your father gets home, we'll discuss it."

Isaiah mumbled something under his breath. All I could hear was, "I don't wanna—"

"What did you say?" I asked.

"Nothin', Ma."

"Go to your room. We'll talk later."

If it wasn't one thing, it was another. Pastor Steele; Alonzo; and now my son wasn't the honor roll student he once was. I didn't know how much more I could take. I wanted so much more for Isaiah, especially since I'd missed out on so many great opportunities. I couldn't let my son follow in my footsteps. I just couldn't. Somehow, someway, I needed to find the strength deep within to overcome whatever it was I was going through, so I could become more involved with Isaiah. Being in my dark place was causing me to lose focus of my son. I couldn't let that happen. But I had no idea how to pull myself out.

My life wasn't supposed to be like this. Within weeks, I'd lost my pastor and my church home, my marriage had crumbled, my health had failed, I'd lost my sanity, and now my son was no longer meeting acceptable academic standards. Why me? What had I done to deserve any of this? And how was I supposed to fix it? I was beyond miserable, with no hope in sight.

Inside, I was crying out for help, but nobody could hear me.

Chapter 14

"Alonzo! I need you to come home now. Isaiah's in trouble," I shouted into the phone. Alonzo had gone to Gold's Gym, and, while he was gone, I had gotten a call from my mom. She and my dad were on their way to pick up Isaiah from his friend's house. Kyon was Isaiah's classmate and basketball teammate, and his parents had caught them smoking marijuana in the basement.

"What's wrong? Is he hurt?" Alonzo questioned.

"I don't think so. All I know is that he was caught smoking weed with Kyon. My mom and dad somehow got the call, and now they are going to pick him up."

"Damn. All right. I'm on my way."

I paced the floor, anxiously waiting for Alonzo, Mom, Dad, and Isaiah to arrive. This recent behavior was so unlike Isaiah—first his grades, now drugs. And Kyon was a carbon copy of Isaiah. He too was an honor roll student who played on the basketball team. He came from what appeared to be a stable, loving home. So to learn that the boys had decided to indulge in marijuana was shocking. Not long after making the call to Alonzo, the front door flew open. I jumped. He had made it home in record speed. Although, granted, Gold's Gym was only four miles from our house. "Is he here yet?"

"No, they should be on their way."

"I can't believe this. Isaiah knows better. We've talked about drug use and why he shouldn't indulge in it. He understands that he doesn't need to get into any trouble right now. This is his junior year. This is the most important year of high school when preparing to go to college. He can't start messin' up his future now. He can't."

Alonzo seemed genuinely concerned about Isaiah's downward spiral. He should've been. This was partly his fault. Had he not been gallivanting around town with that whore, maybe his son wouldn't be acting out right now. Then I blamed myself. I had been so withdrawn and spending more hours in bed than I did with my son, I didn't realize the effects my actions were having on him. Alonzo and I were failing him.

When the doorbell rang, I rushed to the door to let my parents and Isaiah into the house. Both Mom and Dad looked extremely disappointed. Isaiah, on the other hand, looked scared as hell, as he should have.

"Hey, Jaime," my dad said as he entered. My mom and Isaiah followed.

Alonzo walked to the door behind me. "Hi, Mom and Dad," he affectionately called my parents.

"Good evening, Alonzo," my mother said plainly, not in her usual jovial manner.

"Alonzo," Dad said firmly while glaring at him.

This was the first time my parents had come in contact with Alonzo since finding out about his affair, and I could tell they were bitterly cold toward him.

To break up the chill in the atmosphere, I spoke. "Thank you so much for bringing Isaiah home. How did y'all get the call?"

My parents turned to Isaiah, who stood, staring into space. "Tell 'em, Isaiah," Dad instructed.

"I asked Kyon's parents to call them and not y'all."

"But why?" I asked.

"'Cause I figured I wouldn't get in as much trouble with them as I would with y'all."

Alonzo chuckled. "Well, you thought wrong. This is serious, and we will deal with it tonight."

Isaiah asked if he could go to the bathroom before we sat down to talk. When he left the room, my parents explained to us that Isaiah and Kyon supposedly found the marijuana somewhere on school grounds. Instead of turning it in to the school, they came up with the bright idea to smoke it. They thought that because Kyon's parents didn't get home until six, they'd be able to smoke the weed, clean up any paraphernalia or evidence, saturate the house with air freshener, and Kyon's parents would never know. Wrong. Because neither of them had ever smoked before, they got high as kites and literally became stuck on the couch in the basement and couldn't move. When Kyon's parents arrived, not only were they high, but an empty plastic zip bag, a box of cigars, a lighter, and an ash tray were all out in the open. They were straight busted.

After my parents filled us in on what they'd learned from Kyon's parents, they hugged and kissed me good-bye, and nonchalantly told Alonzo, "Good night." There was no doubt that tension filled the atmosphere, and it was thick.

When Isaiah didn't return from the bathroom, Alonzo and I went to seek him out. We went upstairs to find him in his bedroom, lying diagonally across his bed.

"Isaiah. Sit up," Alonzo demanded.

As I stood in Isaiah's room, I admired all the trophies he had won from little league sports and high school basketball. I looked at the endless amount of awards hanging from his walls, including perfect attendance, community service, athletic achievements and honors, citizenship, honor roll, and the principal's award for outstanding academic achievement. Isaiah was such a good kid and extremely intelligent. His recent outlandish acts just weren't of his character. Alonzo and I needed to get a handle at once on what was going on with him.

"What's going on with you?" Alonzo asked.

"Nothin', Dad," Isaiah responded.

"What do you mean 'nothing'? You were caught using drugs today. You better come with something."

"I mean, it was stupid. I shouldn't have done it."

"Nope. You're not getting out of this that easily. Let's start at the beginning."

Alonzo walked over to the desk in Isaiah's room. He pulled the chair over to Isaiah's bed and sat, looking directly at him. I softly sat at the foot of the bed.

"Why didn't you get on the bus today after school? Did you have permission to go to Kyon's house today?'

"No," Isaiah mumbled.

"Speak up," Alonzo bellowed. "If you're man enough to smoke weed, then be man enough to have this conversation. Now, talk so we can hear you. Did you have permission to go to Kyon's house today?"

"No." This time Isaiah was louder and audible.

"So, you took it upon yourself to leave the school and go over to Kyon's house without permission?"

"Yes," he mumbled again.

Alonzo roared, "Speak up."

"Yes!"

Alonzo held up his index finger. "That's mistake number one. You are not an adult. You don't ever go anywhere after school without permission from your mother or me. Understood?"

"Yes," Isaiah responded in a boyish tone.

"Now, whose idea was it to take the marijuana to Kyon's house to smoke it after you found it at school?"

"We agreed together."

Alonzo raised his middle finger. "That's mistake number two. When you found the marijuana at school, you should've reported it. That was not for you and Kyon to take upon yourselves, to walk around your school with drugs. You could be facing expulsion right now if the principal knew that you had drugs on school property and didn't turn it in. Who's to say they weren't your drugs that you brought to school?"

"But they weren't," Isaiah asserted.

"It doesn't matter. It's all about possession, and once you picked them up, you had possession of the drugs, which makes you guilty."

Uh-oh, I thought. Alonzo was dropping the lawyer banter on Isaiah. I hoped this discussion wasn't about to mimic the courtroom.

"So, next you and Kyon go to his house, roll up joints or a blunt, and decide it would be a bright freaking idea to smoke, right?"

"Yes."

"What were you thinking, Isaiah?" Alonzo asked in bewilderment.

"I don't know."

"I don't want to hear 'I don't know.' That's an unacceptable response. I want real answers, and I want them now. So you need to start spilling what I want to know."

"It was just something to do, I guess. Neither of us had tried it before. We were curious and just did it."

"Curiosity? Curiosity? So, you're gonna allow curiosity to mess up your future? We've talked many times about how important your junior year in high school is at this point. From your grades to preparing for the

SAT to possible recruiters from colleges attending your basketball games—you're in a critical stage in your life where your decisions can severely damage the bright future you have ahead of you."

I could sense that Alonzo was growing impatient with Isaiah, so I chimed in. "Isaiah, please tell us what's really going on. There's more to your behavior than curiosity. Your grades have dropped tremendously, you're deciding not to come straight home after school, and now you've been caught indulging in drugs. Something more is going on with you. What is it?"

Isaiah hunched his shoulders. "I don't . . . I mean, I can't really explain it."

"Try," I said tenderly.

Isaiah paused for about three seconds. Then he blurted, "It's this house. I hate coming here. It's just so sad here."

Alonzo sat quietly and observed as I continued to query Isaiah. "What do you mean, 'it's so sad here'?"

Isaiah huffed. "We used to be happy here. We used to be a happy family. Now we're not. It's always dark around here and depressing every time I come home."

He was definitely referring to me. I hadn't let the sunlight shine in our home in weeks.

"And why does that make you not want to come home?" I asked.

"Because I know why it's so gloomy around here. The stuff happening with you and Dad makes me sad too." Isaiah's words instantly broke my heart. In his own teenage way, he was trying to articulate the atmosphere that had been created since the discovery of Alonzo's affair. Just as I'd suspected, my son was acting out because of the actions of his father and his mother, as I had successfully made the atmosphere in his home feel like a funeral home instead of a warm, loving environment.

With a calmer demeanor, Alonzo spoke. "Isaiah, first let me say that I understand your feelings, and you're entitled to them. I agree that things haven't been happy around here for weeks. I'm not proud of what I've done, and I know it can't be easy for you to accept. However, just like I have to take responsibility for my behavior, so do you. What you did today was unacceptable, and you need not make excuses for your behavior. What happened between your mom and me is hard to deal with, I know, but right now I'm working on getting myself together, and I expect you to do the same."

Alonzo paused to ensure he had Isaiah's attention. His eyes seemed to be glued to one spot on his comforter. He gently tapped his leg and said, "Look at me. All families have rough times. Ours will not be spared. However, we need to work toward moving forward as a family. For you, this means getting those grades back up and staying out of trouble. Understood?"

"I understand. I'm sorry, guys. I won't let this happen again, and I promise I will bring all my grades up to make honor roll for third quarter."

I smiled. "Your dad and I love you. No matter what we're going through, we love you. Please don't carry our burdens. We're adults. You worry about a sixteen-year-old's problems. Okay?"

"Okay, Ma. I will."

Alonzo stood to put the desk chair back. "All right, we're gonna hold you to that. No more messin' up. You know if you're messin' up, and I'm messin' up, we put a lot of pressure on your mother. She doesn't deserve that, does she?"

"No, Dad."

"Okay. Then let's start working on cleaning up our acts. I love you, son." Alonzo gave Isaiah a fist bump, and they shared a manly hug.

I walked over to Isaiah and gave him a big kiss on his cheek. I expressed the same sentiments as Alonzo, but I gently informed him that his cell phone, computer, and video game privileges were being taken away for his cannabis stunt. I sincerely hoped that this was the extent of Isaiah's downfall.

I followed Alonzo to our bedroom. I spied him getting dressed. "Where are you going?"

"I'm going to meet up with Everett. This Isaiah thing has got me a little messed up, and I just want to get out for a bit. I hope you don't mind."

I gave him a look that said, "Negro, you lying."

"If you don't believe me call Riah," he defended himself. "She'll confirm. I won't be out long. I promise."

I didn't respond. I had a bit of an attitude because he was running out to hang with the boys at a time like this. I guess he couldn't take Isaiah's admission that he was the reason for the turmoil in our lives. So I figured he was going to wash his sorrows away with a pitcher of beer.

I checked Isaiah's room after Alonzo left, and he was asleep. I felt horrible about not recognizing Isaiah's pain while I wallowed in mine. I needed to make some changes in my life, and fast. The first thing I decided to do was to not return to bed and sleep. Instead, I did something I hadn't done in a long time. I pulled out my Bible—my source of strength.

Chapter 15

Alonzo

"What's up, Everett?" I said, giving him a pound.

"Nothin','Lonzo."

"Thanks for hangin' out, man. I needed to talk to you." I had asked Everett if he could meet me at Bungalow's, a sports lounge. I'd invited Nick out too, but he and London had tickets to a play at the Warner Theater.

"No doubt. No doubt. What's goin' on, man?" Everett asked as we headed toward the bar.

We sat at the end of the bar farthest away from everyone else. The things I needed to get off my chest I didn't want to risk anyone else overhearing. We both ordered Buffalo wings and a bottled Corona.

I usually didn't make a habit of telling my friends about the problems in my marriage, but I was in a bad place at the moment. "I already know you heard from Riah what happened between Jaime and me, but I wanted you to hear from me how things really went."

"I was gonna call you, but I thought it would be best to wait for you to call me. Didn't want you to think I was trying to be all up in your business. I know the story I got from Riah was Jaime's side of the story, which was laden with mad fuel and fire."

"And you know this. I can only imagine the story Jaime's been telling. You should've called, man. We've been friends too long for me to think of you as being all up in my business. I've needed a friend, 'cause I feel like I'm about to lose my mind behind all of this."

"So, that chick in DC broke the rules and forgot to play her position, huh?"

"Exactly. She tried to blow up my spot. Damned chick sent a letter to my house claiming that she couldn't wait until my divorce was final, and how much she loved me and all this other bullshit. She put that shit in a pink envelope smelling like perfume with lip prints on the back. Of course, Jaime sees it, opens it, and that was beginning of a firestorm in my home."

"*Wow*." He placed his hand on his forehead and closed his eyes, like the thought of it pained him. "So Jaime knows about shorty now, huh?"

"Unfortunately, and my life has been hell ever since. Jaime's walking around all depressed, with the worst mood swings ever. One minute she's sad, the next she's trying to act out scenes from the *Psycho* movies and slit my throat. It's wearing on me, man."

"I can understand. You know Riah often threatens to cut off my penis if she ever found out I was cheating. I believe her, too. That's why I can't do it. I just stick to my porn."

I chuckled. "Yeah, at least those anonymous women on the Internet can't see you, don't know you, and won't be sending mail to your house. Anyway, so Isaiah found out about what's been going on."

"Damn. For real?"

"Yeah. Now he's acting out in school, got caught smoking weed, and he acts like he hates me for hurting his mother." Every time I thought about Isaiah, all I could do was shake my head. My son didn't deserve any of this. "Yo, ain't no side chick worth all this drama. I've learned a hard lesson, for sure."

"So, where is Jaime's head right now?"

"I don't know. Sometimes I feel like she hates me and wants me to leave. Other times, I feel like she wants to work on our marriage. I've been doing the guilty man acts of regret and buying clothes, jewelry, cards, and flowers. I've been staying close to home and letting her know my every move."

"So, you're trying to fix it? You're committed to making it work and leaving Candy alone?"

"Hell yeah. I'm done, son. Done. I was freakin' dumb. I have no idea why I consistently want to jeopardize what I have at home for these chicks on the side. It all boils down to sex. That's it. But what else can these women offer besides some ass? Can't nobody hold me down like Jaime. Nobody. And why I keep risking my relationship, my marriage, my family is unbeknownst to me." My second Corona was starting to kick in and I was beginning to face reality. I was extremely sorrowful and regretful.

"Aw, hell. So, you're reformed now?"

"Yes, sir. I'm focusing on making things right at home. These women out here can't offer me nothin'."

"Well, you need to keep doin' what you gotta do to make things right. Jaime's mood is going to be like a rollercoaster ride, so make sure your seatbelt is on tight. You kinda gotta deal with it 'cause you caused it, homie. With time, it should get better. Just keep working on it, and, by all means, lose Candy's number. Don't call her. Don't e-mail her. Don't even think about her. Just be done. She's nothing but trouble. If she's bold enough to send a letter to your house, what else is she capable of doing?"

"You don't have to school me on that. I told you, it's over. I went over to her place and told her that. Her reaction wasn't pretty, but I think she got the message."

"Word? What happened?"

I described to Everett the scene at Candy's house. His eyes widened as I told him how she reacted to my dumping her. Then he shook his head in disbelief when I told him about the leg grabbing stunt she pulled before I left.

"Oh, yeah. Be done with her for real, man. No doubt, she's off her rocker."

I had just finished up my third beer and decided it was time to go. Jaime wasn't happy with my leaving the house anyway, so I figured I'd better at least get back at a decent hour.

"Thanks for letting me vent. I appreciate the advice."

"Anytime, man. Anytime. And remember what I said: run far away from Candy. Far, far away."

"It's already done. Already done."

As I walked to my car, my cell phone vibrated. I knew it wouldn't be long before Jaime called. I had been out a little too long without checking in. I looked down at my illuminated screen. There was a text message, not from Jaime, but from a number not programmed into my phone. I knew the number well. It was from Candy. The text message read: I miss you.

I sighed. Everett's last words replayed in my head. *"Run far away . . . Far, far away."* I deleted the message and headed home to my wife.

Chapter 16

Jaime

I finally mustered up enough strength to shower, get dressed, grab my camera, and drive to my digital photography class. I was looking forward to getting out of the house. This would be a great diversion to get my mind off of all the negativity surrounding me.

When I arrived, I saw my youthful friend. "Hey, Mario. What's up?"

"Good to see you out and about today. I vowed to myself that if you didn't show up for class today, I was going to do a people search for you on the Internet to get your address. Then I was gonna show up at your house and drag you out of bed."

I tapped him lightly on his shoulder and laughed. "Stop playin'."

"I'm not playing. You're my girl, and I hate seeing you in this funk. I just wanna shake you out of it."

"I wish it were that easy. If all it would take to make my life better was a shake, I would've called you weeks ago."

"So, how are things going? Any better?"

Instantly, my mood was saddened. Just the thought of all the turmoil was enough to make the brightest day turn dark and gloomy. I had planned to escape my personal woes by attending class today, but when Mario inquired, I instantly had diarrhea of the mouth. He had always been easy to talk to; therefore, I felt comfortable opening up to him. "No better. If anything, worse. I found out that my husband has a mistress, and I'm harboring more bitterness toward him every day. And my son is now getting into trouble in school and recently decided to roll a joint and smoke it."

"Wow. You really have been through a lot. I'm really sorry things haven't gotten better for you."

"You don't know the half of it," I said, fighting back tears.

"Can I make a suggestion?" Mario asked.

"What is that?"

"I want to do something to make you feel better. When we leave class, can I take you back to my place and make you lunch? As a bachelor, I don't do a lot of cooking, but I know how to make a killer ham and Swiss panini. My mouth has been watering for one all week long, so I picked up the ingredients last night. I'd love to cook you lunch and just try to lift your spirits a little."

I really didn't have anything planned after class but to go home, look at the four walls, and sleep. So I decided to take Mario up on his offer. I needed a change of scenery, and hopefully the company of a friend would help keep me from thinking of my troubles.

After class, I followed Mario back to his apartment in the Tyson's Corner area of Fairfax County. It was a beautiful luxury apartment complex with lush landscape and mature trees, which kept the community hidden from the outside world.

"Take your shoes off," Mario requested when we walked inside.

I obliged, as the white wall-to-wall carpet looked like new. I took a minute to take in my surroundings. It was truly a bachelor's pad because he didn't have any

living room furniture. However, there was a small dining table that sat in the dining room, which had a huge
window. This window allowed too much sunlight in the
apartment for my liking.

"Come in. Have a seat. I don't entertain much, as you
can see. But please make yourself comfortable at the
table. Would you like something to drink?"

"Some water would be fine."

"Water? You're here to relax, for a boost. How about
a glass of wine?"

"Don't be trying to get me drunk. I gotta drive home,
ya know?" I teased.

"I'm not trying to get you drunk. I just want you to
chill. So, is wine okay?"

"Fine. I'll have some wine."

Mario gave me a glass of Moscato. I had never had
it before, but it was good. While I sipped my drink, he
stood in the kitchen to prepare our lunch. "So, Jaime,
tell me. What are you gonna do about Alonzo and his
mistress? Are you planning to stay with him?"

"Every day I think about leaving him. Every single
day."

"What's stoppin' you?"

"I have nothing. If I leave, my only option is to go
back home to live with my parents. I'm thirty-three
years old. I'm too old to be running home to Mom and
Dad."

"You're not too old. If you're being abused mentally
and emotionally, then you need to get out. If your
parents are your only option, then you might need to
make that move temporarily. Too many women before
you have left their husbands and have had to start from
scratch, and they've made it. You can too."

"Mario, you just don't understand. Live life a little
longer, young buck, then holla at me when you have
some wisdom under your belt."

"Um, Mrs. Clarke, don't come at me with that young buck stuff again. Yeah, I may be twenty-five, but I'm no dummy. And I've dated women in their forties. I have wisdom because I surround myself with wisdom."

Damn. I guess he took offense to me calling him young buck. Maybe I should tone that down a bit, I thought. *I thought it was all in fun, but I see now he takes it seriously.*

We chatted a bit more about my marriage until I grew weary of talking about Alonzo. The conversation was draining me, and I wanted to laugh, have fun. As Mario sat down with our ham and Swiss paninis and Caesar salads, I asked him for another glass of wine.

"No more Alonzo talk," I stated firmly. "I came here to enjoy myself, not to have a pity party. You said you were gonna lift my spirits. How do you plan to do that?"

"Just eat your lunch. You'll see."

Mario's lunch was delicious. I thought this was the first time I had eaten anything that didn't cause my stomach to hurt. Or maybe it did, but I was too tipsy to notice. I started to feel a bit lightheaded. My eyes were feeling heavy, like I had an urgent need to go to sleep. It was not a bad feeling at all. It was a good sensation, almost like I didn't have a care in the world.

"Mario," I slurred. "Do you mind if I lie on your living room floor for a minute? I just want to rest my head."

"Are you okay?"

"I'm fine. I just want to rest a minute before I drive home. My stomach is full and the wine has me feeling good. I just want to delight in the moment."

"No problem. Let me get a blanket to put on the floor."

Mario disappeared for a moment and returned with a black-and-white mink blanket. He spread it on his living room floor, and I wasted no time diving on to it and making myself cozy. It was so soft that I knew I'd be asleep within minutes.

"Jaime, when we talked earlier, you said you'd been tense lately. Would you like me to give you a massage?"

With excitement, I replied, "Oh my goodness, yes. I don't know the last time I had one of those."

"I hope I'm not being too forward with this question, but do you want me to massage skin or clothes? If you want me to do your skin, I have a T-shirt and shorts you can put on. I'm not trying to be inappropriate. It's just that in my massage therapy class, I didn't really learn to perfect the craft with clothing."

I really didn't want to take my clothes off at Mario's apartment, but when would the opportunity arise again for me to get a full-body massage—for free? After the hell I'd been through, I needed to alleviate the pain, tension, and stress in the tissues and muscles in my body. Yes, I wanted a full-body skin massage ASAP.

"Okay. Let me get the clothes. Be right back." He returned with what appeared to be a physical education uniform from George Mason University. I went into the bathroom to change.

When I returned, I found that Mario had put on a soothing nature CD that played ocean shore sounds. The atmosphere was already relaxing. I was excited with anticipation.

"Lie down on your belly," Mario instructed. "Relax and try to ease your mind."

The smell of strawberries filled the air. "What's that smell?" I asked.

"The massage oil. Now hush. Let me do my work."

When Mario first touched my back, I could feel the oil's warmth on his hands. Slowly, he moved his hands in an outward motion, then using his fingers and palms, he massaged my back with slow, sensual circular motions. I could feel the muscles in my back loosening instantly.

"That feels *so* good," I said.

"Thanks. I aim to please," he said as he continued to move his hands from an outward motion to an inner circular motion toward my buttocks. "I'm gonna massage your backside now. Is that okay?"

"Backside?" I teased. "If you don't sound like my mom. Go ahead. That's fine," I said without complaint. I was actually looking forward to it. Who gets their buttocks massaged? This was a first for me.

Mario pressed firmly against my cheeks and worked diligently to loosen those muscles. A moan escaped my lips. He then worked his way down to my hamstrings, calves, feet, and toes.

"Turn over on your back," he ordered sensually.

I did as I was told, loving every minute. His hands caressed the soft tissue in my body. This time, Mario worked from the bottom up, starting with my feet, moving his hands way up to the front of my calves and thighs. When he reached my abdomen, I was completely aroused and was nervous about the feelings that had awakened inside of me, but I didn't have the willpower to stop this massage. However, I knew that if it continued, something more could happen.

Using circular motions alternating between outward and inward motions, Mario massaged my abdomen.

"Ooo, Mario," I moaned.

He leaned down and whispered in my ear, "What?"

"You made me horny."

"I'm sorry. That wasn't my plan. Do you want me to stop?"

I didn't answer. I just lay there and let his hands continue to explore my body. He began to cup my breast gently. I moaned again. Mario leaned in and tenderly kissed my lips. He did it a second time, and I kissed him back. The massage had ended abruptly as our tongues were now intertwined.

Mario pulled away and looked at me. "Now you've got me horny."

I smiled. "Well?"

Mario lay on top of me, kissing me slowly and with so much passion. With one hand, he rubbed my throbbing love triangle. I quickly became moist. Mario removed my shirt, and began sliding his shorts down. I unbuttoned his pants and helped him remove his clothing. Completely naked, we lay on the floor, kissing, rubbing, and fondling each other's bodies. Mario grabbed my breasts and sucked my swollen nipples. This was a breaking point for me. I couldn't be teased anymore. I needed to feel him inside me at once.

"I need you now," I said in a sexy undertone.

"I want you too," he replied as he lifted himself from my body. "Let me get a condom."

I was excited about his entrance. Mario eased himself into me, and I let out a moan. His strokes started off slowly, but gradually became faster and deeper. As his pace increased, I let out screams of pleasure, as my body needed this. Each time Mario's manhood would thrust into me, I had feelings of pure bliss. Our unexpected union of ecstasy went on for at least an hour as we continuously rolled around on his living room floor in every imaginable position, until an awesome explosion occurred. We both climaxed and fell into each other's arms. We lay on the mink blanket, quiet, panting, trying to savor the moment.

After about ten minutes of silence, Mario rolled over to look at me. "Jaime, are you all right?"

"Uh-huh," I responded.

"Are you sure?"

"I'm okay. I just think I may need to go now. Can I wash up in your bathroom?"

"Sure. There are clean towels and washcloths in the closet in there. Help yourself."

I was having mixed emotions. I'd have been lying if I said I hadn't enjoyed my time with Mario, but thoughts of just breaking my marriage vows were heart-wrenching. Thoughts of God had run through my mind. I hadn't been in church in a while, but I still knew the Word of God, and I knew that what I had just done with Mario was a sin. I instantly felt like God's heart was crying as his child had committed such a horrible act. Was I now going to hell for committing adultery? Was I even too old to be having sex with this young twenty-five-year-old? I had so many thoughts running through my head as I got dressed in Mario's bathroom.

After fifteen minutes of analyzing my actions, I finally exited the bathroom. Mario had cleaned up the living room and was on the computer.

"Hey, Mario. I'm about to go. Thanks for lunch, the massage, and everything else."

"You seem a little down. I apologize if I took things too far."

"No need to apologize. You didn't do anything that I didn't allow to happen. I had a good time, but I need to get home now."

"All righty, my dear. Well, send me a text when you get home. Just wanna make sure you're okay."

"Will do."

Mario gave me a kiss on my forehead and walked me to the door. I gave a weak smile and waved to him as I made my way to my car. I was sad. Really sad. I couldn't stop thinking about the Ten Commandments and how I just broke commandment number seven: thou shalt not commit adultery.

Chapter 17

Alonzo

I was at work, hidden in my office with the door closed, my face buried in paperwork. I was up against a hard deadline and needed to finish reviewing some information for a case. The office was pretty quiet because everyone had left for the evening. A quiet, peaceful work setting always allowed me to accomplish more work.

A knock came at my office door. Before I could say, "Come in," the person entered. I looked up to see who was interrupting me, boldly entering my office without permission. To my displeasure I looked up to see Candice.

"What are you doing here, Candy?" I bellowed.

She didn't respond. She closed the door behind her. There she stood in my office, unbuttoning her full-length black mink fur, revealing her naked cinnamon skin and black thigh-high boots. She put her hands on her hips and smiled deviously.

For a split second, seeing her plump breasts, perky nipples, flat stomach, and curvy hips sent through my head pleasant memories of our times together, but then reality set in. The woman standing before me was toxic. I wanted nothing to do with her.

I snarled, "Candy, get outta my office!"

"Alonzo, don't front. You know you miss this," she said as she rubbed her hands across her genitalia.

"No. I don't. I thought I made it clear to you that our friendship is over. You need to leave."

Seductively, she walked toward my desk. She walked up to my chair and swiftly swung it around so that I was now facing her. Her naked body then straddled my lap. She pressed her breasts against my chest and held the back of the chair for leverage. "I don't appreciate you not returning my telephone calls, and ignoring my e-mails and text messages."

"Candy, get off me," I said as I squirmed in my executive desk chair.

"Stop fighting it, Alonzo. You know you want me." Candy started licking and kissing my neck. "I miss you, darling."

"I don't miss you."

"I don't believe you," she said, rubbing in between my legs. "We have something special, and you know it. Yeah, I might've jumped the gun in thinking you were getting a divorce. I'm sorry. I misconstrued your actions and words to mean something more. You've got to forgive me."

"I can't. You've made my life a mess. I can't see how I could ever forgive you for—" My words were obstructed by Candy trying to force her tongue into my mouth. I quickly pulled away and turned my head away from her.

"I love you, Alonzo. You know I do. I can't live without you. You have been so good to me. Where in the world would I ever find a man as wonderful as you?"

"That's not my problem. You knew my status when we met. You chose to ignore that. I can't look past that now. My family is in turmoil, and I can't go back. I'm trying to be really patient here with you, but I'm really getting fed up. So, I'm asking you as nicely as possible if you could please get off my lap and leave my office."

Candy grabbed my hand in an attempt to try to get me to touch her private area, totally ignoring my request for her to get out of my office. "Don't you want to see how wet it is right now?"

At that moment, I pushed her off my lap and jumped from my chair. She stumbled backward, but managed to land on her feet.

"Candy, you gotta go now. If you don't leave willingly, I'm calling security. There is nothing more for us to discuss. We're done."

Candy glared at me. Then she looked at my desk. Then she looked back at me. Before I could stop her, with one swoop she knocked everything from my desk onto the floor.

"What the hell are you doing?" I yelled.

She climbed on top of my desk, lay on her back, and opened her legs into the shape of the letter V. "Go 'head, Alonzo. Let me see you call security while I'm lying on your desk, spread eagle. I'll just tell them you were licking my twat. So call 'em."

I wasn't afraid of Candy's threats. I picked up the phone and dialed the security team. "Hi. This is Alonzo Clarke in office 915. I have a woman here I'd like to have removed. Thanks. I appreciate it." When I hung up, I looked at her and said, "They're on the way. I suggest you close your legs, get your ass off my desk, and button up your coat."

I bent down in an attempt to pick up my papers that Candy had thrown to the floor.

"I hate you, Alonzo," she screamed. "I hate you."

"Good. We now agree on something. No need to be in the presence of someone you hate, right? There's the door. Don't let it hit you on the way out."

"Don't be sarcastic with me, you smug son-of-a-bitch," she said, hurling a framed picture of Jaime at my head.

"Oh, my goodness. Now you definitely have to go." I felt myself about to lose control. Security had two seconds to arrive or I was going to do some things to Candy that would cost me my job.

Candy continued to scream like a mad woman, while throwing items from my office at me. I ducked and contemplated if I would tackle her like a quarterback. "You led me to believe it was going to be me and you, Alonzo," she shouted as she threw a stapler at me. "You said we were going to be a family." One of my law books followed. "You told me you loved me," she bawled as she threw my marble nameplate.

Finally, just as she attempted to pick up my fifteen-inch computer monitor, two tall, stocky security officers entered. "I need to have her removed from the building immediately and her name put on the list to not be allowed to return again."

The guards grabbed Candy by her arms, and she struggled with them. Her coat was wide open, her breasts were swinging, and all that was usually left to the imagination was available for security to see.

"Get off of me! Let me button my coat. Y'all ain't getting none of my cookies, so don't be tryin' to look." She snatched away from the guards and scowled at me as she attempted to conceal her naked body.

The team gave Candy two seconds to button her coat before they grabbed her by the arms and escorted her out of my office.

"Thanks guys," I said.

"This ain't over, Alonzo. This ain't over," she yelled as she was being dragged down the hallway.

I closed my office door and sat in my chair. I laid my head back and began swinging from side to side. "What in the hell just happened here?"

It took a few moments for me to gather my thoughts, but once I did, one thing was clear: I had made the right decision in cutting Candy out of my life. It was becoming more apparent that she had psychiatric issues, a chemical imbalance, or something, because she just wasn't being rational. I couldn't believe I had even allowed myself to be involved with someone like that. But it was now over. Hopefully this was the last day I'd have to see her or deal with her antics.

Chapter 18

Jaime

After I left Mario's apartment, I drove around and around, not wanting to go home. After driving aimlessly for a couple of hours, I parked my car on the side of the road for about thirty minutes, just thinking about what I had just done. I then realized that I needed to get home because the sun was going down, and by the five o'clock evening hour in the winter, it was dark. I didn't want to keep riding around unfamiliar roads in darkness.

When I arrived home, I was greeted by an empty house. No one was home. I knew Isaiah would be home late because he was staying after school for tutoring in the classes he had been failing, and for basketball practice. I hadn't heard from Alonzo all day, so I went to check the voice mail to see if he had called.

As I'd suspected, there were two messages from him. The first was at 1:15 P.M. "Hi, Jaime. I just wanted you to know that I am working late on a case. I hope to be home by eight o'clock. Don't worry about dinner for me. I'll grab some fast food. Give me a call at the office. Love you. Bye."

In the recent past, a message like this would have caused me to be suspicious of Alonzo, but because of my own transgressions, I was going to take him at his word. I wasn't going to call the office to check up on him. My focus needed to be getting my head, attitude, and demeanor right before I saw him again.

The second message had come in only minutes before I walked in the door. This time Alonzo sounded distressed.

"Jaime, I'm leaving work now, but I'm not coming home. I'm gonna visit with my dad for a while. I need to . . . I just need to talk to my dad. So I'll be home later. Love you."

Of course, my guilt-ridden self just knew that he was going to talk to his dad because he'd somehow found out about me and Mario. But had that been the case he probably would not have said "I love you" at the end of his message.

I was glad to have the time home alone. I had a lot on my mind, and I wanted to take some time to soak in the bathtub. I needed to rid myself of Mario's scent before Alonzo came home.

I began running a warm bath. I put a couple of drops of bubble bath in the tub and placed my bath pillow up against the back of the tub. I removed my clothing and dipped my big toe inside the water to ensure it wasn't too hot. It was perfect. I slid inside the bathtub and rested my head against the pillow. I exhaled noisily. I couldn't believe this was my life. The more I replayed in my head the day's interaction with Mario, the more I became overwhelmed with disbelief. When I'd woken up that morning, I would have characterized myself as a faithful, loving, honest, and trustworthy individual. By evening, not so much.

Within hours, I had become a part of the statistics I had often heard about while watching *Dr. Phil,* that 30 to 60 percent of all married individuals in the United States would engage in infidelity at some point during their marriage. I never wanted this to be me. I wasn't raised this way. My parents had not set this kind of example for me, and I couldn't figure out why I had set aside my morals and values to engage in such sinful conduct. I wanted to blame the wine; that I'd had too much. I wanted to blame Mario for taking advantage of me at my moments of vulnerability. Then it hit me. My actions were dictated by the actions of another: Alonzo.

As I soaked in the water, I mouthed, "I blame you, Alonzo. This is your fault." Tears began falling from my eyes. I was angry now. I started banging my hand on the side of the bathtub. "Why did you do this to me, Alonzo? Why? I have now turned into you. Your lying, backstabbing, untrustworthy ways have now rubbed off on me. Now, I'm just as dirty as you are. I detest you for this!"

I began washing my body vigorously, almost rubbing off my skin. I continued my tirade, as I was mad as hell at Alonzo, and now I was adding Pastor Steele to the equation. "Had I been surrounded by better people, maybe I wouldn't be an adulterer right now. Wesley Steele, you fake, deceitful, so-called pastor. When you cheated on your wife, what message do you think you were sending to the flock? And you, Alonzo, I never should've accepted your sorry-ass hand in marriage. Maybe, had I married somebody else, I wouldn't be in this predicament now. I loathe you both right now. Both of you."

The more I continued my solo tirade, the more it became clear what the real issue was for me. I wasn't upset that I had betrayed Alonzo. I didn't really care about his feelings. Hell, he never cared about mine. But I was most upset about how God viewed me, and my lack of strength in being able to withstand the negativity around me. Just because Pastor Steele and Alonzo were piss-poor examples of how one should conduct himself in a marriage, that shouldn't have allowed me to fall into the same grimy pit they shared. I was better than this, or so I'd thought.

Isaiah needed at least one role model for how one should conduct himself in a marriage. He already didn't have that in his father. Now, although he didn't know it, he didn't have that in his mother either. This realization was frightening.

As soon as my bath was over, I went into my bedroom to dry off. Mario, the lunch, the massage, the smell of the strawberry massage oil, and the sexual encounter had cluttered my thoughts. My emotions were like a rollercoaster. I was no longer angry, but baffled. I couldn't understand how I could go from beating myself up after the incident, to being angry with Alonzo and my former pastor, to now feeling terrified that I wasn't regretful enough.

Don't get me wrong. I was saddened that I had acted out of character, but my feelings of regret weren't as deep as I wanted them to be. Not once did the need to repent come into my mind. This worried me. I wanted to be so remorseful and disgusted about my encounter with Mario, that thoughts of it would make me want to vomit. But that didn't happen.

In the back of my mind, I wondered if my reason for not seeking repentance was because I was fearful that I was not really ready to completely turn away from the sin. Only time would tell. Only time would tell.

Chapter 19

Alonzo

After the encounter at my office, I was too wired to go home. I was tremendously shocked and agitated by the whole ordeal. I knew if I went directly home after I left my job, Jaime would notice my irritated demeanor. She surely would want to play twenty questions to find out what was wrong, and quite frankly I didn't want to tell her that Candy showed up at my office, naked, with a black fur and hooker boots. I was already walking on eggshells at home, and adding this new twist into the mix would only make things worse.

Instead of going home, I decided to talk to my dad, Howard Clarke. He and I had become extremely close over the last few years following my mother's death. The year after I graduated from law school, my mom passed away from brain cancer. She had fought a long, hard battle before she had succumbed to her illness. On her deathbed, she made me promise two things. One: that I'd marry Jaime and give Isaiah a loving two-parent home. And two: to form a closer bond with my dad. I strived to fulfill her first request, but I had failed miserably. However, I had done well with growing closer to my dad.

My mother used to refer to my dad as her Paul Bunyan, because he was as tall as a giant in her eyes. He had a mocha complexion and wore a beard that covered his face. Although he had reached retirement age, he continued to work every day at the Government Accountability Office as an auditor. He claimed that he loved his job; that was why there was no rush to retire. However, I thought he was a little lonely without my mother, and working kept him busy and interacting with other people.

When I arrived at the house, Dad greeted me at the door with his reading glasses sitting on his nose.

"Hey, Dad. Did I catch you reading?"

"Alonzo. Come on in. Yes, I was reading a *Sports Illustrated* magazine. Nothing important."

We walked into the family room, where Dad had a few books and magazines spread out on the floor. Reading was one of his favorite pastimes. He was sitting in a La-Z-Boy recliner, with the nightly news broadcasting on the television. I looked at the end table and saw a picture of my mom. Seeing her beautiful hazel eyes staring back at me and her big, bright smile always warmed my heart. I felt her spirit in the house every time I went over to visit. I missed her dearly, and I wished she were alive to help me sort through the mess I had made of my life.

"I'm sorry I didn't call before I came."

"Alonzo, my house is your house. You can come over anytime. Your old man ain't never too busy."

I stared at the floor, rubbing my hands together, as I was kind of nervous to open up to my dad about the foolishness I had created in my marriage.

"Son, you look like something is wrong. You okay?"

"Not really, Dad. That's why I'm here. I came to get some advice."

"Okay. I'm listening."

I took a deep breath. This was not easy for me. I had always made my parents proud, but the news I was about to share with my dad would surely disappoint him.

"I kinda messed up with Jaime."

"How so?" he asked, removing his reading glasses.

"Well, I started messing with another woman, and she found out."

"Oh," he said without much feeling.

"And now, my life is a mess. Jaime is a wreck. She's always crying and depressed and walking around miserable. Isaiah found out and now hates me. He started having problems in school and got caught smoking weed the other day."

"Really? Isaiah?"

"Yes, Dad. Isaiah. And now, this other woman, to whom I have made it clear that I want nothing more to do with her, showed up at my office today and caused a major scene. She was naked, crawling all over my desk, begging me to have sex with her. When I declined her advances and told her to leave, she became combative, started throwing things, and I had to call security to have her removed. I don't know what to do, Dad. I feel like my life is falling apart before my eyes."

"Well, son, first let me say that I'm sorry you're going through all of this. It's unfortunate. Before I tell you what I think, let me ask you some questions."

"Okay. Shoot."

"What made you begin this affair with this woman? Were you and Jaime having problems at home?"

I shook my head. "I can't even begin to blame Jaime for any of this. It was me. All me. This affair was simply an ego-based decision. I had a legal case with this woman and began working closely with her. We worked many late nights together, and she subtly began making advances. You know the old saying 'men are only as faithful as their options'? Well, she offered sex, and I took advantage of the opportunity. She boosted my ego, and I enjoyed being with her because it was something new, different, and exciting. Does that make sense?"

"It makes perfect sense. I've been there. I'll just be honest with you. I had a slip-up with another woman when your mother and I were first married. It was early on—way before you were born. I never got caught, but I came close, and I was scared to death. The thought of your mother finding out scared me straight. So I'm not here sitting in judgment of you. I know how you feel."

I was a little shocked that my dad had indulged in infidelity as well. I wondered briefly if infidelity was in my genetic makeup. Then I quickly released the thought because the difference between my father and me was that at least he'd had sense to get his act together and not make the same mistakes repeatedly. "So, what do I do?"

"Do you still want your marriage?" he asked.

"Yes, I do," I affirmed.

"Good answer. There's nothing out here, Alonzo. Nothing. I'd tell any young person today that if you've got a good woman by your side, do everything in your power to make it work. You may think the grass is greener on the other side, but it isn't. Believe me, it isn't. You and Jaime need to talk, talk, and talk. Communication is key. I know you probably hate harping on the subject and being the target of her venom, but it makes her feel better to vent about it. She wants to get her feelings off her chest. And since you messed up, you gotta endure it. Also, along with Jaime, Isaiah has got to be a priority. That boy should not be suffering behind the actions of his father. So you need to find every way possible to earn his trust and respect back. You don't want him to grow up scarred by this. If y'all think family therapy will help, then I suggest you hop on it fast. But whatever you do from this point on, never forget that your family is your main concern. Not the Department of Justice, not your friends, not me, and definitely not this other woman. And speaking of her, what's her name?"

"Candice Barr. She works for HUD in DC."

He raised his eyebrow and smiled. "Oh, really? She works for HUD? Well, you know, we can call her boss at HUD to inform them of her shenanigans." My father had many connections within the federal government. He had everybody of importance on speed dial. "If she wants to keep up this lunacy, we can and will have her stopped. You just give me the go-ahead, and I'll do it."

"I'll let you know. Right now, I'm trying to handle it as best I can. There's no need to get anyone else mixed up in the situation since I made the stupid decision to get involved with her."

"It wasn't the best decision, Alonzo. But instead of beating yourself up about it, you've got to figure out how to move past this and make things better. Stop living in the past and look toward the future. If you want to save your marriage, then you need to make the necessary steps to do so. You're a smart guy. Do your research. Find out what you need to do to help get things back on track. You can never go wrong with seeking God and finding a therapist."

I leaned my head against the back of the sofa. I sat there, letting his words of wisdom sink deep into my brain. I listened attentively as he continued to help guide me through the valley.

"The only other piece of advice I can offer you, son, is to let this be a learning experience. I know the temptation out in the world is great, but these women are not worth risking your marriage—your wife, your son. You don't want to mess things up with Jaime for a temporary piece of tail that's not guaranteed to stick by you for better or worse, richer or poorer. Jaime has. You don't want to be that man who ruins his marriage and finds himself in his mid-to-late forties, spending lots of weekends alone and trolling for dates, instead of going on family vacations, celebrating holidays with your family, and just having feminine energy around you. Take it from a widower: you don't want to go to bed solo after spending years with a woman by your side. It can be lonely."

That was deep, and I most definitely got the message he was sending. "Dad, I appreciate this talk. You have helped me out a lot. I will continue to focus on my family, and do what I need to do to make things right— even if it pains me. I'm a lawyer. I'm used to fighting, but this fight is so much more important to me than any other case I've ever argued in court."

"I'm glad I could be of some help to you, son." He lightly patted me on my back as I walked toward the door. "Keep me updated with everything and please call or come by if you want to talk some more. I'm here for you, son."

I turned to hug him. "Love you, Dad."

"Love you, son."

Chapter 20

Jaime

Isaiah had called ten minutes ago and said that a teammate's parent was bringing him home from practice. I hadn't cooked a thing. After the day I'd had, I didn't feel up to it. Alonzo was going out to grab a bite to eat, and I didn't have an appetite, so I decided to run out to get Isaiah's favorite chicken sandwich combo from Wendy's.

I rushed out to get Isaiah's dinner in the hope of making it back home before he did. I went to the drive-thru window, ordered, and hurried back home. Alonzo's car still wasn't in the driveway, but I could see Isaiah's bedroom light on.

I grabbed my purse and the Wendy's bag and soda, then walked toward the front door. As I approached, I notice something hanging from my doorknob, but because it was dark I couldn't make out what it was. I bent down to inspect the object. It was something with red and white lace. *I know this isn't what I think this is.* I put my purse on my shoulder. I held in my left hand the cup and bag containing the food. With my right hand, I removed the strange, oddly placed item from my door.

I jumped and dropped it. "What the hell?" I shrieked. "Who in the hell put those on my doorknob?"

I was livid. I'd come home to thongs, sexy thongs, hanging from my front door. I knew with 100 percent certainty that those were not my thongs. It didn't take a rocket scientist to figure out who the trifling culprit was who would commit such a vile act.

I knew Isaiah was probably starving inside, so I decided to play it cool. I entered the house and called him. "Isaiah. Hi, baby. I've got your dinner."

Isaiah rushed down to get his dinner. "Thanks, Mom," he said before taking his meal back up to his bedroom.

In front of Isaiah, I appeared to be as cool as a cucumber, but inside I was hot as fire. There were only two people I could directly link to these thongs—Alonzo and his trick! As soon as Alonzo got home, he would have some serious explaining to do.

I waited, fuming, for Alonzo to get home. As soon as I saw his car pull into the driveway, I ran to the front door. When he walked in the door, I threw the thongs in his face. They hit him directly in the nose and fell to the floor.

Startled, he looked down to see what had just attacked his face. "What the hell is wrong with you, Jaime?" he growled.

"What the hell are those, Alonzo?" I mimicked his voice.

"I don't know. You tell me."

"I went out to get our son some dinner, and I came home to these thongs hanging from the doorknob. They sure as hell ain't mine. So whose are they?"

"I have no idea."

"Are they yours? You wearin' girly panties now?"

"Hell, no."

"Then tell me what's going on, Mr. I Want My Family And I'm Going To Do Better."

Alonzo didn't respond. Instead, he looked around the house. He whispered, "Where's Isaiah?"

"Upstairs, eating. Why?"

"Come on. Let's talk."

We went downstairs into the basement. I guess this was his way of ensuring that Isaiah wouldn't hear us arguing. I knew I shouldn't have attacked him when he walked through the door, knowing Isaiah was home, but I was heated about those panties, and I wanted answers. Not to mention, I didn't notice them when I left home, and Isaiah didn't mention anything to me about them when I brought his food in the house. So, the perpetrator had to have put them there when my child was home alone and could have been possibly watching my house, waiting for me to leave to pull such a stunt. This thought was alarming.

"Sit down. Let me talk to you about something," Alonzo said. "I just came from having a long talk with my dad about this very issue. I'm at a loss about this whole situation and don't really know how to handle it. I needed someone with good judgment to talk to, and my dad gave me some really good suggestions. He told me to keep an open line of communication with you as we continue to endure this hardship. So I want to tell you about something that I didn't want to tell you before. I also think what I have to say will give you some clarity as to why those thongs were left on the door."

"Tell me what?" I had a major attitude.

"Candy is behind this scheme. She's mad at me. Ever since I told her I was done with her and wanted nothing more to do with her, she's been hounding me. She continues to call my job and leave voice mail messages, and she sends e-mails and text messages that I don't respond to. Today, she unexpectedly showed up at my office, demanding to speak with me, inappropriately dressed, and I had to call security. She became irate when I told her I was going to have her removed from my office, so she started throwing things and causing a big scene. Finally, the security team showed up and escorted her out of the building. Now, a few hours later, there are thongs on the door. There's no doubt in my mind that she's behind this. This is just her way of trying to sabotage our marriage. We can't let her win, Jaime. We can't."

I offered no sympathy. "This is all your fault, Alonzo. If you hadn't gotten caught up with this psycho then maybe our family wouldn't be enduring this right now. This broad is writing letters, showing up at your job, now at our house. When does it stop? You sure know how to pick 'em."

"I know this is my fault. I'm not denying that. I'm working on fixing this. I really am," he said sincerely.

I got up to walk back upstairs. There was no need to continue to talk to Alonzo at this point. I was too bitter to even empathize with him, however genuine he may have been. Candy was wreaking havoc on his life, our lives, and I blamed him for it. Because of his lack of control and lustful nature, he'd brought her into our world. Now we were all suffering behind it. I was pissed—really pissed.

"Jamie," he called, following me up the stairs. "Can we finish talking, please?"

"There's only one more thing I have to say," I barked. "You created this hell we're living, and all I know is you better fix it and fix it fast."

"But, Jaime, that's what I'm trying to do—"

Suddenly, Isaiah appeared out of nowhere. "Mom, Dad," he yelled. "Would you please stop fighting?" Then he stormed back upstairs and slammed the door to his bedroom.

Chapter 21

"Oops! I did it again," I sang while lying in bed with Mario, both of us completely nude. This visit was just like my last—three glasses of wine, a good meal, and an excellent workout session. Mario and I had graduated from the blanket on the living room floor to Mario's king-sized bed. We had lots of room to roll around in the sheets, and he had just rocked my world.

The unrelenting stress in my life was definitely taking its toll and my stomach aches and irritable bowel issues were still very much present; however, the time I spent with Mario seemed to temporarily repair my emotional and physical duress.

"So, you're a Britney Spears fan?" he teased.

"Nope. I just think the lyrics are fitting. Honestly, the last time I was here, I didn't have any intention to return. I wasn't proud of what you and I had done. I didn't really want to go down that road again."

"What changed your mind?" he asked as he propped pillows behind his head.

"The scene last night at my house."

"What happened?"

"I think Alonzo is still messing around with that woman, Candy. Out of the blue, a pair of red and white thongs appeared on my doorknob. He admits he thinks it was one of her schemes. But why? She had to have been trying to send a message."

"Or she could just be deranged and trying to stir up trouble," Mario said, seeming to side with Alonzo.

Not in agreement with him, I rebutted, "Or she wanted to let me know that those were the thongs she had on while she was with my husband, or that he purchased them for her."

"Oh, Jaime," he retorted.

"Oh, Jaime, nothing. There was a message in those panties being on my door. It's not totally clear, but there's some sort of significance.

"So, a pair of thongs is what led you to call me today and give me this treat." He smiled, rubbing my thighs under the sheets.

"Yup. Why should I continue to be faithful to Alonzo when he's still out playing around? He keeps talking about how he wants his family and his marriage, but this chick won't disappear. Until I have proof that she's gone, and he's no longer involved with her, I'm gonna do me. As long as I suspect Alonzo is out doing his thang, then I'm gonna play the game as well. If he can roll around with trollops and think it's fine, then I'm gonna have my fun too."

Mario joked. "Well, if it's fun you want, I'm happy to oblige."

I liked Mario. Our intimate friendship caused me to wrestle with an array of emotions. Sometimes I felt justified and other times I felt guilty because I knew better; I knew the Word of God. However, oftentimes, my flesh won the wrestling matches, as I was overcome with feelings of revenge against Alonzo.

I appreciated Mario for accepting our friendship for what it was—friends with benefits. Nothing more. He knew without me saying it that he was my boy toy. I wasn't looking for a relationship, but just somebody to go to when things at home got tough, and I wanted to relieve some stress. He and I both knew this wouldn't last forever, but we agreed we'd have fun for the moment.

Changing the subject, Mario asked, "It's Friday; what are your plans for the weekend?"

"Tonight, my girlfriends, and I are hangin' out at the National Harbor. Alonzo is supposed to be doing a guy thing with his friends, so he says. Isaiah will be spending the evening with my cousin London's son, Gabriel. What are your plans?"

"My friends and I are going to Atlantic City for the weekend. So I'll be out of town. But if you need to get in touch with me, you can always call my cell."

"Do you promise to win lots of money for me?"

He laughed. "Only if you promise to let me lick you up and down one more time before you go."

I rolled over on my back and Mario climbed on top of me. I closed my eyes and allowed him to take me to ecstasy.

Later that evening, London, Riah, and I were at National Pastimes at the National Harbor. The waiter brought a basket of bread to our table and asked for our drink and meal orders. London seemed to be displeased with my drink selection.

With a scowl she asked, "So, you're not eating, but you're drinking wine?"

"I'm gonna eat," I said, grabbing a roll from the basket. I opened up a butter packet and began to spread it over the bread. Riah and London looked at me as if I had lost my mind.

"What?" I laughed.

"So, let me get this straight. Wine, bread, and butter is your dinner for tonight?" London asked.

"Yes. My stomach has been hurting a little today. There's no need to order a meal because I'm not going to be able to eat much of it."

Riah chimed in, "Your stomach hurts, you won't eat food, but you'll drink alcohol? I'm confused."

"Don't be. Don't worry about it. I'm good. Y'all enjoy your meals and let me enjoy my bread and wine. Isn't that what they serve in church on Communion Sundays anyway?"

Riah and London burst into laughter. "Girl, you silly," London joked.

The waiter came back with our beverages. I knew I'd want a second glass of wine, so I ordered it right then. I didn't even look at Riah and London because I knew they were frowning at my choices, but I didn't care. I just wanted to drink.

"So, what's up with y'all? How are things?" I asked, hoping to distract them from questioning me about my alcohol consumption.

"Nothing much here," Riah said. "Just working and working and working. Oh, but a colleague recommended her church to me. She has been begging me to visit for weeks now. I talked to Everett about it, and I think he's up to going."

"That's great. Where is it?" London asked.

"It's in Woodbridge, Virginia. Not far from Potomac Mills."

"After you visit, call me and let me know what you think. I may want to go with you, if you decide to return," London stated to Riah.

"I sure will. How about you, Jaime? Would you like to go?"

I frowned and shook my head. "*No,* my sister. I can't do the church thing right now. I don't trust anybody. Can't see me going to anybody's church anytime soon."

London said, "I feel ya, but you can't lump all pastors into the same category. Yes, Steele is a fraud, but you can't hold his actions against every preacher."

"Speaking of Wesley Steele, have y'all heard the latest about him?" Riah queried. London and I both said that we had not. "Chile, First Lady Steele moved out the house and has filed for a divorce."

London gasped.

I was full of glee. "Good for her! He is a sorry bastard."

"Not only that, but a lot of the members have left the church. The ones who are still there are the old folks who don't know how to turn on a computer, let alone go on the Internet to see the video of him and that woman. Besides, y'all know, older folks are dedicated to their churches. The only way they'll leave permanently is if a hearse is carrying them away from there."

I was curious about the others who had stayed. "Besides the older generation, who else stayed? None of the young folks are still there, are they?"

"Well, you got some people who still trust him and believed him when he said that it wasn't him in the video."

"What?" I snapped. "He said it wasn't him in the video? You've got to be kidding me." I guzzled the last little bit of my wine after hearing that news. I needed the waiter to bring me glass number three.

"Yes, indeed," Riah affirmed. "Ol' Wesley pulled an R. Kelly and said it wasn't him in that video. Word is, he stood before the congregation and told them he had been set-up, that the video was edited and put together to make it appear to be him, but it wasn't."

"And people believe that?" London looked perplexed. "I mean, did the church members really fall for that story? Really?"

"Some did," Riah confirmed. "That's why they are still there. Sad, but true."

"They are so foolish. If that wasn't him in the video then why did his wife leave him? Why is she filing for divorce? She wouldn't be taking such drastic actions if he was really a victim of sabotage in this case. Are they that gullible?"

London shrugged. "I'm guessing they aren't putting two and two together."

"What about the deacon board? Couldn't they have stepped up and kicked Steele out of the pulpit?" I questioned.

London chuckled. "Word on the street is that Spirit of Truth is an independent church run all by Wesley Steele himself. Somehow, years ago, he was able to convince the members of the deacon board to relinquish control of the church to him. The change was comparable to a city council telling the mayor he could make all future decisions without its input."

"Are you serious?" Riah exclaimed. "What in the world did he say to get them to give up control?"

"That's the million dollar question," London said. "But I hear it's happening in lots of mega-churches. I bet if you do some serious research on a many of these 'celebrity' pastors, with these huge congregations, private jets, million dollar cars and homes, you'd find that they all are operating independently."

"As well as operating as pimps in the pulpit," Riah added.

"That too," London agreed. "Shoot, many of these pastors seek the independent church route so that they are not bound by the bylaws requiring them to have boards in place to serve as checks and balances in church governance. That's why Wesley Steele is still able to mock God in the pulpit and carry on as if he hadn't been literally caught with his pants down. He thinks he's untouchable."

As Riah and London ate their crab cake meals and I sipped my drink, we talked a little more about Pastor Steele before the conversation turned to Alonzo and me. I had not disclosed to London and Riah my relationship with Mario. I didn't want them to sit in judgment of me. Besides, this fling with Mario would be over in a hot minute. I just needed something to do to take my mind off of Alonzo's disloyalty to me and our marriage.

"I haven't had a chance to tell you all about yesterday. I came home to find thongs hanging on my front doorknob."

"What the hell?" Riah exclaimed.

"Yeah, girl. So, when Alonzo got home, he told me he thought his jump-off had done it because she's mad at him for ending things with her. She also showed up at his job yesterday, acting a fool, and he had to call security to have her removed. He thinks the thongs were payback for having her kicked out the building."

"That tramp is out of order." Riah was heated. "For real. She messin' with the wrong folks now. How dare she come to your house? Your house!"

"She better not let me catch her in the streets," I said. "I definitely have her listed as number one on my beatdown list. She is beyond disrespectful."

London seemed concerned. "You all need to be careful. She seems unstable. I'm not liking what I'm hearing about this—" London's cell phone rang. She dug in her purse to find it. "Oh, it's home calling." She answered it. "What! Oh, my gosh. Oh, my gosh! We're on our way."

I looked at her, puzzled. What could possibly be going on?

She flipped her cell phone closed. "We gotta go. We gotta go. That was Nick. He said we need to come home. Isaiah and Gabriel have gotten into trouble." London made a gesture toward the waiter. "Check, please! We really need to go."

Instantly, a sharp pain entered my stomach. I didn't know what was going on, but when I heard that Isaiah was in trouble, all I saw was this image of my baby in jail, in a five-by-nine cell, peeking through steel bars. At this point, I was thankful his father was an attorney.

Chapter 22

After receiving that frightening phone call at the restaurant, London, Riah, and I bolted to London's car. We hopped in, and she put the pedal to metal as she sped on 495 South to hurry home. When we arrived at London's house, Nick, Everett, and Alonzo were all there sitting at the dining room table, looking bewildered.

"What happened?" London said as she ran over to Nick. "Are the boys all right?"

Nick responded, "They're safe. They haven't been harmed, but both of them are pissy drunk."

"What?" we shouted in unison.

"It seems that Gabriel and Isaiah thought it would be a good idea to go into our wine cellar and treat themselves," Nick stated. "When we got home we called out for them, but they didn't answer. After we searched upstairs for them and they weren't there, we went into the basement. There, we found an entire bottle of Bacardi Limón empty and the boys passed out on the floor."

"It scared me at first," Alonzo said. "I didn't know what had happened. When we called their names, they were unresponsive. That's when Nick noticed the liquor bottle on the table along with two cups. Looks like our boys decided to get smashed tonight. Now they're passed out."

"I'm gonna kick his ass," London spat. "Gabriel knows better. When the hell did he start drinking? He's never been interested in going into our wine cellar before. Now, all of a sudden, tonight he wants to experiment with alcohol?"

Gabriel was a good kid, just like Isaiah, but considering the path that Isaiah had been going down, there was no doubt in my mind that it was his idea to open up that bottle of Bacardi.

"I'm so sorry, y'all. Had I known that Isaiah was going to come over here and do this, I wouldn't have left him home for the evening," I said apologetically.

"It's not your fault," Nick said. "Gabriel knows better. Whenever he wakes up, he's going to never even think about taking another sip of alcohol again."

Alonzo chimed in, "Oh, I hear ya, bruh. Isaiah is on punishment for life. He too knows better."

Alonzo and I went down into the basement to awaken Isaiah. When I walked down the steps, all I could see was my son and his teenaged cousin stretched out on the floor, lying flat on their stomachs, drunk and snoring. I was so disappointed in Isaiah.

I walked over to Isaiah and shook him. He moaned and turned over. I tried to wake him again, but to no avail.

"Watch out," Alonzo said. "Isaiah, get up now," he said as he yanked him from the floor.

Isaiah was excessively impaired, but Alonzo didn't care as he forced him to gather what little faculties he had and walk up the stairs. After a few stumbles, Isaiah reached the top of the steps. I was overcome with shock as everyone watched my stumbling, drunk son make his way to the front door.

"We're leaving now," Alonzo said. "We're gonna take him home and skin him alive as soon as he wakes up. Sorry this happened."

"No apologies. I'm just glad they're okay," London said. "Jaime thought they were in jail or something. You know as mothers we always think the worse."

We said our good-byes to London, Riah, Everett, and Nick, and made our way to the car. Isaiah snored all the way home, with drool coming from his mouth.

Upon arriving home, Alonzo carried Isaiah into the house and directly into his bedroom.

"Do you think we should get him out of his clothes and put on his pajamas?" I asked.

Alonzo frowned. "Hell, no. Let him stay just like that."

Isaiah coughed. He then rolled over. Alonzo and I thought he was waking up. We stood there watching him with sadness in our eyes, as we were so disillusioned by the sight of our son, inebriated. Isaiah coughed again. He sat up, opened his eyes, and then suddenly he began vomiting all over his bed and the floor. After he finished, he lay back down and went back to sleep within seconds. I was totally disgusted.

"What should we do?" I asked.

"Let him sleep in his own vomit. Tomorrow, he will have to clean up that mess. It's not our job to do so."

Alonzo and I walked out of Isaiah's room and closed the door. I hated seeing my baby like that. It was extremely disheartening to see his life unravel right before my eyes.

I went into the computer room to check my e-mail. I was hoping that maybe Mario had sent me a flirty message from Atlantic City to help put a smile on my face. When I logged on, I saw that I had one new message from a Candice Barr. My eyes widened from the surprise of seeing her name in my inbox. How in the world had she obtained my e-mail address, and what reason would she have to be sending me any type of messages?

The subject line read: Alonzo Clarke likes bondage.
My heart raced. My palms were instantly sweaty. I
knew this wasn't going to be good, but curiosity forced
me to click on it anyway. There was no message, just a
photograph attached. I clicked on the picture and fury
engulfed me. The image was of a naked Alonzo with
a swollen penis, lying on his back, handcuffed to the
back of a headboard. I recoiled and cupped my mouth
from the shock of seeing this photograph. And, as if the
photo being sent to me weren't bad enough, I almost
died when I noticed the list of names and addresses
of other people who'd received the e-mail. In horror,
I read each name, including that of my mom, dad,
Alonzo's dad, London, Nick, Riah, Everett, and several
addresses that ended with ".gov," which were without
doubt Alonzo's colleagues in the federal government.

"This bitch," I screamed as I printed the incriminating photo of my husband.

I stormed out of the computer room to find Alonzo.
He was in the bedroom, watching television. I walked
over to him and threw the picture. He sat up and yelled,
"What's wrong with you now?"

"When you lie down with dogs, you get up with
fleas. That tramp you're fucking is now sending nude
photos of you to all our friends, family, and to your
colleagues. How could you be so stupid? Why would
you allow her to handcuff you to the bed and take your
picture? I swear, sometimes with all that book knowledge you have, there is absolutely no freakin' common
sense. Now, I've got to deal with the embarrassment of
my friends and family seeing my husband naked and
bound."

"I . . . I . . . I never posed for this picture," Alonzo
stammered with a look of dismay spread across his
face.

"Well, then the whore set your ass up good. And don't say it isn't you because you and I both know it's you."

"But I don't get down with handcuffs, Jaime. You know that. You ain't never seen me do no bondage type stuff."

I gave him a look of repulsion. "Alonzo, I don't know what the hell you do with your other women. Obviously you *do* get down with handcuffs 'cause the proof is in your hands."

"But this has to be—"

"Save it, Alonzo! Just save it. You make me sick. This is the stuff I'm talkin' about when I say you only think about yourself when you go out and break your marriage vows. You have no idea how many lives you are affecting for a few minutes of pleasure. If you stop letting your penis guide your thoughts, and use the brain in your head, then maybe stuff like this wouldn't happen."

"Jaime, I know you're upset. Understandably so, but I'll take care of this immediately."

"The damage is done. That message can't be recalled once the send button was hit. Ugh. I'm tired of this. All of this. I'm too pissed off to stay here right now. I'm leaving."

"Where are you going?" Alonzo demanded to know.

Sarcastically, I responded, "To hell if I don't pray." I dashed out of the bedroom, down the stairs, and out the front door. I needed a drink—a strong drink.

I sent Mario a text message saying, i wish u were here :). I hated that he was in Atlantic City, because I really didn't have anyone else to run to. I found myself sitting alone in a small tavern about five miles from my house. I'd never envisioned myself going to a bar to drink alone, but I was stressed and too angry to stay in the house. Isaiah was at home drunk, and within the next twelve hours my relatives and peers would be opening their e-mails to find a picture of my husband handcuffed, exposing his genitals and proof of his infidelity.

It may have sounded self-righteous of me to come down so hard on Alonzo about his affair after my romps in the sack with Mario, but at least my indiscretions weren't circulating around the Internet. Alonzo and Candy's affair was far more detrimental to folks than the two times Mario and I had been together.

I gulped the Patrón Pineapple beverage I'd ordered and closed my eyes. The feel of the liquor hitting the back of my throat caused a gag reaction, as I was not used to drinking hard liquor. I decided to slow down a bit and sip little by little. "Hello. Is this seat taken?" I heard a male voice say.

I opened my eyes to see a handsome specimen standing before me, with a tan complexion, curly hair, and light brown eyes.

"No, it's all yours," I said, more friendly than normal. I usually didn't talk to strangers, but tonight I guess the alcohol allowed me to loosen up a bit.

"Thanks," he said. He extended his hand to me and introduced himself. "My name is Sebastian. And yours is?"

"Jamie." I cringed immediately. In my younger days, there had been an unwritten rule saying that I never gave strangers my real name in bars or clubs.

"Nice to meet you, Jaime. What are you drinking?"

"Patrón Pineapple," I sang. The liquor was already taking effect.

"Do you mind if I order you another one?"

"Aw, thanks. That's awfully nice of you. I'd like another one." Each time Sebastian spoke, my eyes were glued to his lips. They had a slight plumpness and looked exceptionally soft.

"So, what brings you out here all by yourself this late? It's a little after midnight. Shouldn't you be at home?"

I rolled my eyes. "Home is the last place I want to be. I'm staying here until they put me out."

"If you don't mind, may I ask why?"

With handsome Sebastian by my side and second drink in hand, I began to feel real comfortable—too comfortable. I developed loose lips and told Sebastian everything about my home life. Moments before the bar closed, he knew everything from Alonzo's affair, to that trick Candy's antics, to Isaiah being a straight-A student, to his grades dropping after learning about his father's affair. I cleverly left out anything about Mario. I still had to keep that part of my life hidden from everybody.

Sebastian shared with me that he was in the DC Metro Area for business, but would be flying back to Detroit the next day. He was single with no kids.

Our conversation was quite enjoyable. We chatted, we laughed, and we flirted. I even asked him if I could touch his lips, and he agreed. As I'd suspected, they were as soft as marshmallows.

"Sebastian, the bar is going to close soon. Looks like they're cleaning up. I want to thank you for the drinks and the conversation."

"It's been my pleasure. It's definitely been nice chatting with you, as well."

"Well, I'm gonna go to the bathroom before I leave. Then I'm gonna head home."

Slyly, he said, "Can I help you take your panties off?"

I looked at him as if I'd misunderstood what he said. "What did you say?"

With a devilish look in his eye, he said, "You said you have to use the bathroom, right?"

"Yeah."

"Well, can I help you take your panties off?"

I stood there, baffled. I had never had such a request before. It was strange, but the thought of it was exciting. "Sure. Come on."

The bar was relatively empty, as it was closing time. Inconspicuously, we walked toward the bathrooms. First, I entered the ladies' room. Shortly thereafter, he followed, so as not to draw attention to ourselves. I went into the largest stall in the bathroom—the wheelchair accessible stall at the end. Sebastian was right on my heels. He locked the door and looked underneath to see if anyone else was in the bathroom with us. He whispered, "We're alone."

He grabbed me and kissed me while unbuttoning my jeans. I reached for his belt buckle and followed suit. He slid down my pants and white lace panties all at once.

"Turn around," he said.

I obliged as I heard him rapidly rip open a condom wrapper.

Slowly, he bent me over, arched my back, and inserted himself in me. I jumped as he plunged his manhood into my inviting hole. He was in complete control as he dug deeper and faster inside me. "Ooo, this feels so good," he moaned as he pumped with everything he had.

"Give it to me," I whispered. I wanted to scream in delight, but I knew I was in a public place, so I bit my bottom lip instead.

"I'm about to . . . Ahh," he said, quickly withdrawing from me.

I turned to face him, redressing myself. "Thanks for that. It was enjoyable."

"No, thank you."

Sebastian exited the stall first. I heard him run the water at the sink, and then he left the restroom. I then left the stall, washed my hands, and left. When I went back to my space at the bar, I found money for the bill and Sebastian's business card. On the back was a message that read, "Call me if you're ever in Detroit."

I had no intentions of calling him. He was just a one-night stand. Nothing more. Had Mario been in town, I would not have given Sebastian the time of day. He was just my five-minute option for the night.

Now, after the thrill of having illicit bathroom sex with a stranger, I had to go home to Alonzo's nude photo and Isaiah's drunkenness. The Clarke household was a total wreck. We needed help, and fast.

Chapter 23

After my late-night bathroom tryst with Sebastian, I arrived home to find Alonzo asleep and Isaiah still passed out in his own vomit. I was glad neither of them was awake because I didn't want them to see the letter "S" I had stamped on my forehead for my scandalous behavior at the tavern.

Instead of sleeping in my bedroom next to Alonzo, I crawled into the sofa bed in the family room. The real reason I didn't want to get in my own bed was because I was afraid I smelled like Sebastian's juices, but my excuse to Alonzo would be that I was upset about that nude photo that Candy had sent to everybody in the Washington Metro Area.

It felt like I'd had two hours of sleep before my home phone and cell rang incessantly. When I didn't answer, my cell chimed, indicating that I had either a voice mail or text message. I knew exactly why people were blowing me up so early on a Saturday morning. And now the culprit was staring me in my face.

"Why did you sleep down here last night?" Alonzo asked in a foul mood.

"I needed my space. I was angry, and I wanted to be alone."

"So, where were you last night?"

"Out."

Alonzo puffed out his cheeks. "Jaime, please don't play with me. I'm really not in the mood for games today."

"I went for a ride. I wanted to clear my head. I needed to think of how I would deal with the abundance of calls I'd receive today about that e-mail. I'm pretty stressed about it. I'm ticked at you, but really, I would never want you exposed like that."

"Thanks. I appreciate that. I've been in contact with some folks to figure out how to handle this legally. The people at my job who she sent the e-mail to are not high-level folks, just colleagues at my level—people I would consider my friends at work. So, they're cool. I talked to my dad, and he's following through with his threats to contact her supervisor at work."

"Really?" I was surprised.

"Yeah. I didn't get to tell you all the details about the conversation with my dad because you were so angry about the panties on the door, but he wanted to put a stop to her foolishness as soon as I told him. I told him no because I wanted to handle it. But now he says he's on it no matter what I say. Oh, and I called your parents this morning. I talked to your mom. I opened up to her about everything. She said she and your dad wouldn't even open the e-mail. So, I guess that leaves London, Riah, Nick, and Everett. I really don't care if they see it."

Stunned, I said, "Wow. You called my mom? And opened up to her about us?"

"Yeah, I did. I love your parents, especially your mom. She's the closest person I have to a mother since my own mother died. I noticed the distance between us the night she brought Isaiah home from Kyon's house after that weed smoking incident. It bothered me that your mother was upset with me. I wanted to reach out to her, but decided to let some time pass. Your parents have always been fond of me and supported me, so to even think that they look at me differently for hurting their daughter bothers me. I know opening that horrific e-mail would probably only cause more of a division in the family, so I reached out to them. When I called, your mom answered, and we had a long, long talk. Despite my actions, although disappointed, she was very encouraging and promised me that neither she nor your father would even open the e-mail."

My mother always found a way to display just how much of a Christian she really was. I wished I had more of her characteristics. "That was nice of her."

"Indeed it was. She even prayed with me on the phone before we hung up. And she said she had faith that we would overcome this storm we're in right now."

"Did you tell her about Isaiah getting drunk?"

"I told her, but she already knew because London told her mom, and you know the sisters talk. She was saddened to learn about it, but she said that he should be the reason we should fight harder for our marriage. Look, I'm trying. I'm willing to do all I can, but you've got to work with me, Jaime. I understand that it's not easy to just forgive me overnight, but I think you've hardened your heart. It's like you have an ice pack in your chest where your heart used to be. You gotta work with me. I can't make this marriage better by myself."

"It's just not that easy, Alonzo. I've been through a lot with you, for a lot of years. I can't just sweep this under the rug like before. I'm tired and, quite frankly, I'm afraid to forgive you and move forward. Every time I let my guard down with you, you shatter it again. I can't keep putting my heart at risk. The pain is just too much to bear. I'm not saying I'm not willing to try. I just can't move at your pace. It'll be when I'm ready. Besides, the fact that this tramp Candy keeps making appearances one way or another isn't helping me overcome this. It just keeps reopening the wound."

"I feel ya. I'm just asking that you don't give up on us. I know I've messed up. I'm the one who caused the turmoil, so I can't dictate the healing process. I'll be more considerate of you needing more time to heal."

"Thanks. I appreciate it." I was sincere in my response. I really did want him to step back and give me time to work through all of this. Just because he *now* decided he wanted to be a good husband and father didn't mean I was supposed to instantly and eagerly jump on board. He'd spent years being deceitful, so now he had to be patient in his quest for forgiveness. It just might take weeks, days, or years.

In the middle of our conversation, we heard movement above our heads. Isaiah had risen from the dead. It was now time to take him outside in the backyard, have him pick his own switch, and give him a whooping he'd never forget.

"Are you ready to talk to Isaiah?" I asked Alonzo.

"Come on, let's go," he said, distressed. Ending one intense conversation to go directly into another was something neither one of us was looking forward to.

"Isaiah," I called. "Come down into the kitchen." Alonzo and I were seated at the kitchen table, awaiting Isaiah's entrance.

Isaiah entered the kitchen with squinted eyes, shuffling his feet.

Sarcastically, I asked, "Is it too bright in here for you?"

"A little."

"Good." This was one time I made sure all the curtains and mini and vertical blinds were open, allowing the sunshine to pour into our home. I wanted him to endure every ounce of pain and misery associated with a hangover.

"Have a seat," Alonzo ordered. Isaiah did as he was told.

Struggling to find the words, Alonzo began to speak. "I'm at a loss here. I mean, I don't . . . I don't know what to say to you. It wasn't that long ago that we sat you down after the marijuana stunt. Now you're drinking alcohol. What the hell is your problem?"

Isaiah did his normal hunching his shoulders, holding his head down, looking at the floor, but Alonzo wasn't having it.

"Pick your head up!" Alonzo was angry and the look on his face made me a little nervous for Isaiah. "Open up your mouth and talk. First drugs, now alcohol. What were you and Gabriel thinking last night?"

"Well, we just wanted to try it. We had heard about kids playing a drinking game in school and thought it would be fun. I didn't know it was going to make me feel this bad. My head hurts, and my stomach is upset. I'm sorry. I know it was stupid."

"Damn right it was stupid," Alonzo spat. "There's such a thing as alcohol poisoning, you know. You and Gabriel could be in the hospital right now. The two of you didn't think at all."

"Isaiah." I spoke warmly. When Alonzo was coming down hard on him, I found it always hard to be combative with him as well. "I know things have been difficult for you lately, but the way you've been acting lately is not the answer to your problems. You've got to make better decisions, baby, because the path you're on is a dangerous one. Drugs and liquor at sixteen years old is not the direction you should be going in. What can we do to help?"

"Nothing," Isaiah replied.

"There's got to be something. We are your parents. We love you. We want to help you. How can we make things better for you?"

"I don't know." Isaiah seemed awfully pouty, and I believed in my heart that he had more he wanted to say, but was afraid to open up. I was fighting against typical teenager behavior.

Alonzo, still fuming, interjected into our conversation. I didn't think he had the patience for the softball treatment I gave Isaiah. "Well, while you try to figure out what the problem is, let me ask you a few questions. Like I said before, we've talked about the problems within our family. We agreed that we were all going to make the attempt to move forward. Instead of you moving forward, you get into trouble again. This is now your second time. Maybe I didn't make myself clear the first time about our expectation and how you needed to clean up your act. So, is there something we need to clear up? Something you didn't understand from the first conversation?"

"No, Dad. I understand. There won't be any more problems," Isaiah affirmed.

"I agree. This is the last time." Alonzo pounded his fist on the kitchen table. "Your behavior is totally unacceptable, and we won't stand for it. Now, I'm gonna say this for the last time: stop the bull crap! Get your act together, get your head on straight, and bring back the old Isaiah. Got it?"

"Got it," he mumbled.

"First strike: marijuana. Second strike: alcohol. Third strike: you're out! Now, take that however you want to, but know I'm not playing."

Isaiah looked up at us and asked, "I'm punished, right?"

"Uh, yeah." I looked at him as if he were still drunk for asking that question. "So, besides no cell phone, and no computer unless it's for school purposes only, make sure you hand over your iPod. There will be no video games and only two hours of television each day. No calls on the house phone, either, and no afterschool activities unless it's basketball. Basically, you have no life until you can show us that you have brought your grades up, and when we stop getting phone calls about you being drunk or high."

"But, Ma—"

"I don't wanna hear it. Until you produce the old Isaiah, life as you know it is no more. Now, go upstairs, clean up that nasty vomit, change your bed sheets, and write a letter of apology to London and Nick. After that's completed, you need to work on any homework you have due for school."

When Isaiah left the kitchen, I glanced at Alonzo. "I hope he gets it together," he said.

"Me, too," I replied sorrowfully as I laid my head on the kitchen table. I felt badly about the mayhem we'd created in Isaiah's life. It was hypocritical of me to berate Isaiah for his behavior when I needed to clean up my act as well. If his struggle to better himself and to stay out of trouble was anything like mine, I could identify with the difficulties he endured in his attempt to correct his behavior. It was hard, but the desire for change needed to be present. I wasn't sure about Isaiah's position, but I hadn't made it to the point where I desperately wanted to change. Hopefully, I'd open my eyes sooner rather than later.

Chapter 24

A month after Isaiah's drunken stupor, Alonzo's incriminating photo, and my sexual rendezvous with a complete stranger, things hadn't gotten any better in the Clarke household. Isaiah was still on lifelong punishment, which caused him to walk around the house as if he were angry with the world. Alonzo had slowly but surely stopped showering me with cards and flowers. I guess he had grown tired of me not responding the way he wanted me to.

Springtime had arrived, and not only did it bring about warm, sunny days, green grass, and blooming flowers, but it also brought about more pain, suffering, and abandonment of my morals. I didn't admit it to anyone, but I began to drink alcohol excessively when Alonzo and Isaiah weren't at home. This was my attempt to cover up the mental anguish I felt for participating in such despicable acts. When I looked in the mirror, I didn't know who I was anymore. I almost felt like I had become a sex-crazed alcoholic who was acting out of pain and crying out for help, but had no one to turn to. Therefore, I turned to Mario for comfort. Seeking relief from him only increased our "sexcapades." And while I indulged in excessively naughty behavior, my abdomen pain and loose stools didn't get any better, either.

My mom had grown tired of me complaining about my stomach issues, but not doing anything to address the problems. Since I was neglecting my health, she took it upon herself to make a doctor's appointment for me with her digestive doctor. When I met with him, he had no immediate answers about the symptoms I had described, but suggested I have two procedures: an upper gastrointestinal endoscopy and a colonoscopy. The gastrointestinal endoscopy was a visual examination that would enable doctors to see my esophagus, stomach, and the first part of the small intestine. The colonoscopy was a procedure used to see inside of my colon and rectum. Because I had to be sedated for the procedures, Mom accompanied me.

A week later, I was headed back to the doctor's office to obtain the results. I was a bit edgy because I was unsure of the outcome, and, of course, I had a glass of wine before leaving home to help calm my nerves.

"Good morning, Jaime," said Dr. Austin: a Caucasian, older gentleman with a head full of white hair. He was very kind and had a wonderful bedside manner.

"Good morning."

"How are you feeling this morning?" he inquired.

"Okay, I guess. I'm a little nervous about the results."

"But, other than that, how are you feeling physically? Any effects after the procedures last week?"

"No, not really. Nothing out of the ordinary. The same pains; no better, no worse."

"Oh," he said while flipping through my chart. "Well, after reviewing your results, it looks like you have Crohn's disease."

A little confused, I asked, "What kind of disease?"

Very kindheartedly, he replied, "Crohn's disease. It's a chronic inflammatory disease of the intestines and can affect the digestive system anywhere from the mouth to the anus."

I still wasn't clear after his explanation. "I don't . . . I don't really understand."

"Well, it's like everything along your digestive tract—your mouth, stomach, small intestines—is swollen. In your case, the results show problems with your stomach and small intestines. There are ulcers in your stomach, which definitely contribute to the stomach burning, and your small intestines are swollen, which is why you had difficulty with your bowels."

"So, ulcers and swollen small intestines aren't good, are they?"

"No. Not at all. When intestinal swelling occurs, it restricts your other body functions. In your case, it's your bowels."

"What causes Crohn's disease?" I quizzed.

"Scientists have many theories about what causes Crohn's disease, but none of them have been proven. So the exact cause is unknown."

"Is there a cure? How can I get better?"

"Well, Jaime, there is no cure; however, it can be controlled. With medication and the proper diet you can live with Crohn's, and it can even go into remission."

"What kind of medicine will I have to take?"

"Since your results show a mild to moderate form of the disease, I want to start you off with a milder medication called Pentasa. And I'll prescribe Prevacid for the stomach ulcers. The Prevacid should only be temporary, but the Pentasa may possibly be a lifelong medication."

Cautiously, I asked, "Dr. Austin, do people die from Crohn's disease?"

He smiled. "As with anything, people can die, but you are going to be fine. There have been some Crohn's-related deaths; however, you won't be one of them because we are going to make sure you are taking care of yourself. We're not going to worry about dying, but how you're going to live a perfectly healthy life with Crohn's. So, since we're on the topic, the number one thing you should know is that stress is a killer. Stress can make Crohn's symptoms worse. If you're surrounded by a lot of chaos, you want to work to start alleviating that from your life."

Inwardly, I chuckled. *Chaos? In my life? Drama and stress are at the center of my life.*

Dr. Austin went on to educate me about Crohn's. He told me that I needed to exercise regularly, get a sufficient amount of sleep, and maintain a healthy diet, because certain foods would trigger inflammation in my small intestines. I couldn't smoke, I had to be careful of certain over-the-counter medications, and the biggest lifestyle change was to avoid alcohol as much as possible, because it could not be mixed with my medications used to treat the disease. That information alone was a shock to my system. How could I live without my wine?

I left the doctor's office with loads of information and pamphlets about the illness to further educate myself. I wasn't happy to learn that I had a chronic illness. However, I was thankful it wasn't something worse. At least this was a condition I could live with. That is, if I did what I was supposed to do to remain healthy.

When I arrived home, I walked over to the phone to call my mom to give her the results from the doctor, but before I could dial her number, the doorbell rang.

"Yes, may I help you?" I said to the delivery man standing at my door with the most beautiful bouquet of flowers.

"Hi, I have a delivery."

I beamed. "Sure. I'll sign." I figured that Alonzo hadn't forgotten about sending flowers after all. And to think these came at such a great time—a time when I was a little down after receiving the news about Crohn's disease.

I walked into the kitchen, and I placed on the counter the vase that held a dozen gorgeous assorted roses, forming a rainbow of colors. The bouquet instantly filled the room with happiness.

Attached was a card. I gently removed it from the stick nestled into the floral arrangement. I opened the envelope and began to read the card aloud:

> *Dear Candy,*
> *Just sending beautiful roses to thank you for the beautiful night we had together. I'll never forget last night. Thanks for making me smile again. It's been awhile.*
>   *Love, Alonzo*

I closed my eyes and squeezed them tightly. Then I opened them again, peeking at the card, hoping that this time it would read, "Dear Jaime." But it didn't. The flowers were *not* for me. Either Alonzo was a complete jackass for sending flowers to our home for this tramp, or this was another one of Candy's extreme measures to get his attention.

Instantly, I was enraged. So much for not being stressed. I snatched the flowers from the vase, ripped them to shreds, and threw them on the floor. I ran upstairs, grabbed a duffle bag out of my closet, and started throwing panties, bras, shoes, and toiletries into the bag.

"I'm sick of this! I can't take this anymore! I gotta get out of here," I cried as I continued to throw clothes into my bag.

After I quickly packed, I grabbed my purse, my keys, and I left. I didn't know where I was going, but I was getting the hell out of the house.

Chapter 25

My cell phone was on fire: nonstop ringing, text messages, and voice mail messages, all from Alonzo, London, Riah, and my parents. I even saw numbers I didn't recognize. I disregarded them all. I didn't want to talk to anyone. I was hurt. Here I was dealing with the aftermath of learning I had a sickness that I would probably have for the rest of my life, and, if that weren't enough, I was then greeted at my front door with flowers for my husband's mistress. None of the people calling my phone could understand my position. All they'd do was try to diminish the situation and attempt to pacify me. I didn't want to hear that, so I ignored all calls and messages. I wasn't going home. I had other plans—plans that led me in the opposite direction of my residence.

With a tear-drenched face, I knocked on the door of my comforter and waited patiently.

"Jaime? What are you doing here?" Mario was surprised to see me.

"I'm sorry I didn't call first. I've been riding around for a while now, trying to decide where to go, and . . . and I found myself here."

He stretched out his arm and wrapped it around my neck. "Come on in. What's wrong?"

I walked into the home that had become so familiar to me. I had spent many hours at Mario's apartment within the last few weeks, so when I walked in, I instantly made myself at home. I kicked off my shoes, walked over to his dining room, sat down, and placed my head upon the table. Mario walked over and began to massage my shoulders.

With genuine concern, Mario asked, "Jaime, please tell me what's going on. Why are you crying?"

"I'm sad. Really sad, Mario," I sobbed.

Mario passed me a few tissues. "Why, sweetheart?"

"Because today I had my follow-up appointment with my doctor."

"That's right. I forgot about that. How did that go?"

"Okay, I guess. I'm not dying, but he told me I have Crohn's disease."

"Oh, I've heard of that. It's like having irritable bowel syndrome, right?"

"Something like that. Crohn's disease affects my bowels and other areas of my digestive tract. I also have ulcers in my stomach. I have to take medication for the rest of my life if I don't want it to get progressively worse."

"Wow. I'm sorry to hear that. But let's focus on the positive, because the diagnosis could've been worse. Thank goodness it's something manageable. You can control this disease."

"Yeah, that's what the doctor said. I gotta eat right, exercise, get lots of rest, and try to avoid stress."

"You're not doing a good job of avoiding stress right now. You seem pretty tense to me. Is it just the diagnosis that's got you upset or something else?"

I sat up and looked at Mario. With his fingertips, he wiped my tears away. "No, there's more."

"What else?"

Just the thought of the roses and the card made my tears flow faster. "When I got home from my appointment, a delivery man showed up at the door with flow-

ers. I assumed they were for me from Alonzo. I thought
he was sending me a nice floral arrangement since
he knew today was my follow-up doctor's visit and he
hadn't sent flowers in a while. But when I opened the
card, it was addressed to Candy from Alonzo, stating
how much he enjoyed last night, and how it had been
awhile since he smiled."

Mario gasped. "Jaime, stop playin'."

"I'm dead serious."

"But he wouldn't do that. Think about it. Why would
your husband send his jump-off flowers to his address?
I've heard of being sloppy, but nobody is *that* sloppy.
This sounds fishy to me."

"You think so?"

"Hell, yeah. Your husband is too smart for that. I don't
have a good explanation for what happened, but I just
can't believe he would be stupid enough to mix up the
address of his wife and his chick on the side."

"It doesn't matter, Mario. Whatever the explanation,
it doesn't negate the fact that this whole ordeal is foul."
I was crushed. I had already dealt with enough, and I
wasn't up for another one of Alonzo's rationalizations
as to how or why the flowers were sent and how or why
I received them. "I'm sick and tired. Sick and tired.
I just wanted to get out, so I packed a bag and left. I
drove around for a while and my car led me here."

Mario sat on the floor in front of my chair and began
massaging my feet. "Jaime," he said, "you know you're
more than welcome to stay here if you want."

"You don't mind?"

"Nope. Where's your bag?"

"In the car."

"I'll go get it."

I gave Mario the keys. While he was gone, I looked
at all the missed calls on my cell phone. There were

thirty-three of them. I had made up my mind that I wasn't calling anyone back. I'd deal with Alonzo and my family later. I just wanted to be left alone to wallow in my grief. I powered down my phone and didn't plan to turn it on again until morning.

Upon Mario's return with my bag, we headed to the bedroom. "Come lie down," he said as he waved me over toward the bed. I slowly walked over to the bed and sat on the edge. Mario sat beside me and held me tightly.

"Tonight, no sex. Let's be intimate without inter-course. I want to just lie down, talk, hold you, and calm your stress. Is that all right with you?"

I smiled. "That's perfect."

I made myself comfortable in Mario's arms and basked in delight as we talked about nothing of importance. But, as we conversed, he soothed my spirit, and we cuddled—something Alonzo used to do, but hadn't done in a very long time.

Chapter 26

"Where the hell have you been?" Alonzo yelled as soon as I stepped foot in the door. To my dismay, he hadn't gone to work—probably because he was worried all night about my well-being. I'd expected him to be upset, but I was greeted by a seething fury-filled Alonzo. The anger on his face was so pronounced that I expected to see his eyes turn red, and to see fire shoot from his ears at any moment.

I wasn't moved by his irritation, so I responded nastily, "Hangin' out with a hooker named Candy Barr."

Alonzo rushed toward me and chest bumped me as he got directly in my face. Immediately, my sarcastic demeanor turned to fright. I thought he was going to hit me.

With his index finger pointing in my face, he bellowed, "Don't you fuckin' play with me! This is not a game. You stay out all night long, not answering your phone, and nobody knew where you were. You had us all worried. Your mom was just minutes away from calling the police to report you missing. Nobody slept a wink last night and you have the audacity to come in here with this smug-ass attitude? How dare you? Who the fuck do you think you are? Now let me ask you again, where were you?"

This time, with Alonzo standing in my personal space, I decided not to give a smart-aleck response. "At a hotel," I lied.

"Which one?" he questioned with a tone of skepticism.

"The Alexandria Inn," I nervously replied.

"How'd you pay for it?"

"With cash."

"Where's the receipt?" he demanded, holding out his hand.

"In the trash. Why?" I felt cornered by his questioning. He was a lawyer. He was good at cross-examinations, so I had to try to flip the script. Backing away from him, I exclaimed, "You have some nerve. You don't have a right to question me about anything after I received those flowers yesterday addressed to your *girlfriend*."

Alonzo walked up on me again. Using his index finger again, he aggressively started poking the side of my head. "Where is your brain, man? Where is your brain? Can't you see an act of sabotage staring you in the face? Think about it. Would I really send Candy flowers to *my* address? Really?"

"I don't know. You don't always do your own ordering. I know this. How do I not know your secretary didn't order the flowers and sent them to the wrong address instead?"

Alonzo shouted, "Because I don't work with incompetent people who would do such a thing. You can try to spin this however you'd like to make yourself believe that I actually did this, but you know damn well I wouldn't have sent those flowers. It's another one of Candy's schemes, and you fell for it. Instead of calling me at work or waiting until I got here to discuss it, your irrational, emotional ass leaves the house and goes MIA."

Alonzo had made some valid points, almost similar to what Mario had said. Maybe I should have called.

Maybe I should have waited to hear his explanation. However, I would never admit to Alonzo that I over-reacted. I was too ticked off with him to agree with him. Had I been more rational in my reaction, maybe I could've gotten different results.

Alonzo paced, his body still full of fury, and his rant continued. "I came home yesterday, eager to find out about your doctor's appointment and the results of your exams. Instead of finding you, I was greeted by poor Isaiah who looked like he had seen a ghost. When he came home from school, he was baffled as to why there were a bunch of shredded flowers all over the floor, and his mother was nowhere to be found. Of course he called your parents, and they came running. It was just one big mess. Thank goodness your parents took Isaiah and had him stay with them so I could con-centrate on finding you, but we were all concerned—worried sick about you, especially Isaiah."

Once again, I had failed my son. In my rage, I never stopped to think about Isaiah coming home to find the flowers all over the floor. I never considered that my staying out all night would cause him to think that something bad had happened to me. I felt horrible—but only for what I had done to Isaiah. I didn't give a rat's ass that Alonzo was up all night, distressed. He needed to be. Now he knew how I felt every time he walked out the door. The anxiety and fear that he was with another woman was always there—always.

In a calmer manner, Alonzo said, "Jaime, don't ever do that again. No matter what is going on between us, don't just roll out and not contact anyone to let them know you're safe. I'm glad you're home and that you're all right."

I could've offered an apology at that point, but I didn't. I was still heated that he thought it was okay to jump up in my face. He didn't have the guts to do that when I had that knife in my hand a couple of months ago.

"Do you want me to call your parents, London, and everybody to let them know that you're home safe, or do you want to do it?"

"You can do it," I snapped, and walked away.

"Jaime," he called.

"What?" I said with an attitude.

"Last night was your second disappearing act. I'm not getting a good feeling about it, and I don't like it. I'm letting you know now that the next time this happens, when you return I'll be gone."

"What's that supposed to mean?"

"It's one thing to have an argument, leave, go for drive, and be gone for an hour or so, but to stay out all night, not answer your phone, and do things of that nature is unacceptable. All I'm saying is that you've done it twice. I'm not accepting a third."

"I didn't stay out all night before," I defended myself.

"The night you stormed out of here after you got that e-mail with my picture in it, you left here a little before midnight and by two A.M. you still weren't home. Then, whenever you did creep back in here, you slept downstairs. Sounds awfully suspicious to me. Look, there's no need for a long discussion about it. I'm just letting you know up front. I have feelings, too. I've made my mistakes, but, dammit, I'm trying, and if you can't jump on board then I'm jumping off. Plain and simple."

I got a little uneasy when I heard Alonzo talking about leaving me. I wasn't prepared for that. I wasn't going to let him know it, but he had me a tad bit shaken with his statement. I wouldn't admit it to him, but I got his message loud and clear. However, I was still going to play the tough role. "Whatever, Alonzo. You just want an excuse to leave anyway."

"Not true. I'm not getting into a long discussion about it. I've said my piece. I hope you've heard my message. I'm glad you're home. Now I can get some sleep after I call your folks. You can go upstairs now and do what you gotta do."

Did this Negro just dismiss me? If so, that wasn't a problem. I was done talking to him too.

"Hey, Jaime," he called again.

"What?" I sighed under my breath. *Didn't he just tell me to go upstairs? Didn't he have phone calls to make? Didn't he want to sleep? What? What? What?*

"I know things got a little heated between us, but I'm still interested in what the doctor said yesterday. Do you mind telling me? If not now, maybe later?"

Sarcastically, I snapped, "The doctor says I'm dying. Start planning my funeral."

Chapter 27

Alonzo must have taken my comments about dying seriously. I assumed that when he called my family and friends to inform them that I had returned home safe, he also told them I was about to pass away. The next day, my family unexpectedly showed up on my doorstep.

My father, acting strangely, arrived at my door without warning, asking if Isaiah could stay with him for the evening. He also had Gabriel with him. He claimed that he and the two boys were going to hang out, do some male bonding. I hoped that bonding included a firm lecture about their recent drinking episode.

A few moments after my dad left with Isaiah, another unanticipated knock came on my door from three visitors: my mom, London, and Riah. Alonzo was gone. Isaiah was all of a sudden with my dad and now these three were at my house without notice. Something was definitely going on.

"Hi, Jaime." My mother greeted me with a hug and kiss. "Sorry we didn't call first, but we wanted to surprise you. We brought dinner."

Riah and London followed my mom in the house, both wearing cheery smiles and carrying covered dishes. I actually didn't mind the company. It was better than being home alone, but I knew there was a hidden agenda behind this visit.

"I'm starving. What did y'all bring to eat?" I asked, rubbing my growling belly.

Mom responded, "I baked lasagna. Riah made tossed salad and brought various dressings, and London stopped at the Cheesecake Factory and got three hunks of delicious plain cheesecake with strawberry topping."

"Hmm, that sounds good. Let me get some plates."

The four of us piled lasagna and salad on our plates, then sat at the dining room table and Mom said grace. Immediately afterward, our forks dove into the food. For a minute it was quiet, kind of an awkward silence, until Riah spoke first.

"The lasagna is good, Mrs. Paula," Riah said with a string of cheese hanging on her chin.

"Yes, Aunt Paula, this is delicious, as is the salad," London added.

The small talk was killing me. It seemed like everybody wanted to say more, but nobody wanted to be the first one to speak up, so I did.

"Hey, y'all, I want to apologize about yesterday. I know I had everybody worried. That wasn't my intent. I was upset and wanted to be alone. Hopefully, it will never happen again, but if it does, I will be sure to at least let one of you know that I am alive and well. I promise not to have you all that concerned again. I'm deeply sorry, and I hope you can forgive me."

"I appreciate your apology, Jaime," my mom affirmed. "You had us all worried. Poor Alonzo was scared to death. He was almost out of his mind."

I rolled my eyes and hissed.

"Why did you roll your eyes?" Riah asked.

"Because he's full of it. I don't believe he was that concerned. It was probably a front he put on for y'all."

My mother disagreed. "No, Jaime. I talked to him, and I saw him. He was pacing the floor, anxious and scared. He was only as calm as he was because Isaiah was around. It wasn't an act, baby."

"Why would you doubt his concern for you?" London asked.

"'Cause he's the reason I stayed out all night long. I know y'all already heard about the flowers coming here for that tramp Candy from Alonzo. How disrespectful can he be?"

My mom laughed. "Chile, you can't let that girl get you all worked up. She sent those dang flowers. That thing is a miserable soul right now because Alonzo don't want her no more. He wants his wife. So, what does a jilted woman do? She goes above and beyond to cause trouble, hoping to get the man back. What she doesn't realize is that her antics only pushed him away further. If there was ever a chance Alonzo was going to creep the streets with her again, he surely won't do it now, 'cause she's shown that she's absolutely crazy. You can't fall for the bull, Jaime. You've got to be stronger than that."

"I hear you, Ma, and in hindsight, I realize now that it probably was Candy. But you all have to put yourself in my position. Alonzo has been unfaithful for more years than he's been faithful. All I know is his betrayal, backstabbing, and lies. So, it's not beyond reason to think that he would do something like send flowers to Candy."

"Jaime, I think you need counseling," London suggested. "Every time the subject of Alonzo or your marriage comes up, I see the pain in your face. You've dealt with a lot over the years, and I don't think you've ever healed from the first occurrence. Without ever getting over the first act of infidelity, you've had to endure the same treachery time and time again. In my opinion, you're scarred in ways none of us really know, and it's time for you to get some help."

"I agree," Riah chimed in. "You seem really unhappy. You haven't been yourself lately. I feel a sense of detachment from you that I've never felt before. I miss my old friend and I want her back. I think if talking to someone will assist you with dealing with your pain, then I want you to do it. I'll even go with you, if need be."

Finally. The real reason behind this unexpected visit. This was a mini-intervention to plead with me to seek therapy. Thus far, they had made some legitimate points, but I wanted to hear everything they had to say before I agreed with or refuted their ideas.

It was now Mom's turn to give her lecture. "I think Riah's assessment of your behavior and demeanor being different is accurate. I've seen it too, but I noticed it before the Alonzo situation. Your spirit was broken after the Pastor Steele incident. I think you were more devastated than anyone really knew. Then Alonzo's skeletons came flying out the closet, Isaiah's troubles started, and then your health became an issue. You've been through a lot since the beginning of this year, and it's enough to make anybody have a breakdown. I want you to seek therapy as well, but my greatest desire is for you and your family to get back into church. Even through all of your trials, the Lord hasn't given up on you. Please don't give up on Him."

"Everett and I visited a really nice church recently. Let me know if you're up to visiting. Maybe we can go one Sunday."

I nodded. "I appreciate all your concern for me. I really do. I concur that I have changed, and I'm unhappy. Some days I feel really good, and other days I'm depressed. I want to see a therapist, so I'll look into it soon. Now, as far as the church thing, that may take more time. I know that not all pastors are the same,

but Wesley Steele has caused me to not trust anyone
for the moment. Give me more time on that one. I miss
church. I miss being active in church. I miss my family
going to church. But I'm just not there yet. And as far
as Alonzo goes, I'm not ready to forgive him. He's hurt
me far too many times, and I'm not being duped into
his deception anymore. I don't trust him, and I'm not
so sure he's really vested in making things better in our
marriage. Just like with church, I need more time."

"Jaime, I understand your need to protect your heart,
but I want to share with you some of my pillow talk conversation," London teased. "Nick says from his conversations with Alonzo, he appears to be extremely remorseful
about his actions."

"Oh, my gosh," Riah interjected. "Everett said the same
thing. His exact words were, 'That chick must have him
shook 'cause he more committed to his marriage than
ever before.'"

"See, Jaime?" London continued. "I think your open
wounds aren't allowing you to see the possibility that
Alonzo is genuine in his quest to change."

"Honey, you've got to give him a chance—maybe just
one more chance," Mom advised. "But don't take my
word for it. How about you seek the Lord, and I mean
really seek Him, on this matter? Okay?"

"Okay, Mom," I agreed half-heartedly.

"Now, I don't mean to change the subject," Mom
said, licking her lip, "but I want a slice of cheesecake,
and I want to know about your visit with Dr. Austin."

As soon as we poured the strawberry topping on
my cheesecake, I explained the diagnosis of Crohn's
disease. My mom had heard of the illness before, but
Riah and London had lots of questions. Sadly, telling
them about the treatment, the things I needed to do to
maintain a healthy lifestyle, was the worst thing I could

do. They were going to be on me like white on rice to ensure that I was doing all the right things to stay well.

"Well, I'm thankful you have answers now and that it's nothing too severe. You'll be fine. Your support system will make sure of it." Mom winked. I knew that she too was going to be all over me.

"By the way, I love Dr. Austin, but he's only going to give you the prescription drug choices. I want you to consider taking some natural supplements that are beneficial for the digestive system. I'll do the research and get back to you."

"Thanks, Mom. I appreciate it."

After we devoured the dessert and felt ten pounds heavier, we cleaned up the dining room. Riah came up with a suggestion.

"Hey, y'all. Since it's still early, the men are hanging out, and Isaiah and Gabriel are with Mr. Ben, would you all like to go to the movies to see *Madea Goes to Jail?*"

"That's sounds like a great idea," my mom said. "I wanted to see that movie, but there's no way I could get Ben to go with me. He refuses to go see Tyler Perry dressed up like a woman."

We all laughed.

"I'm up for it. I'd love to get out of the house and do something fun," I exclaimed.

"Let's go look up the movie times on the computer," London said. "Maybe there's a show starting soon."

As we prepared for our girls' night out at the movies, I felt really good to be surrounded by such a great group of women—my mom, my cousin, and my dear friend. I was grateful that they cared enough about me to intercede on my behalf. I definitely heard their points of view and was receptive, but it was just like I told Alonzo: my healing process was on my time and not anybody else's.

Chapter 28

Alonzo

While Jaime spent the evening connecting with the ladies in her life, I decided to hang out with the guys. I invited Everett and Nick over to my dad's house for some male bonding. Not only would this give me an opportunity to spend time with my dad, but this also helped me escape all the madness going on at home.

Since none of us were experts in the kitchen and didn't have a great desire to cook, we arrived at my dad's house with three boxes of pizza, two bags of chips, one bag of pretzels, and a case of beer.

"Dad," I called out to him as I put my key in the door to let myself in. "It's me, Nick, and Everett."

"Come in, guys. I'm in the living room."

As always, Dad was lounging in his favorite place in the house.

"Good evening, Mr. Howard," both Nick and Everett said.

"Hey, guys. How you doing?"

"Doing well," Nick responded. "How about you?"

"Oh, I'm fine. Can't complain," Dad responded.

"Thanks for having us over," Everett said. "It's rare we get time away from the women, so this was a nice gesture."

"No problem at all. You know you all are more than welcome to come over here anytime. It's just me in this big old house by myself with nobody to talk to but the television. So I don't mind a little company."

I hated that my dad was lonely. I always had mixed feelings about him moving on with another woman because I loved my mother dearly, but I thought it was selfish of me to want him to stay alone without a companion for the rest of his life.

"Dad, I'm gonna put the pizza in the kitchen."

"You can leave it right here. We don't have to go in the kitchen. We can sit right here and eat in front of the flat-screen television."

I grabbed paper plates from the kitchen and a bottle opener. Shortly thereafter, the guys and I were chomping on cheese, meat lover's, and chicken supreme pizzas. We were eating like we hadn't eaten in days.

"I want to thank y'all for getting together. I've had a lot on my mind lately, and I just wanted to get some male insight. I don't want to dampen the mood with my problems, but I need some help."

"What's up, son?" Dad asked as he hit the mute button on the remote control.

"Well, I think Jaime's having an affair."

"Get out!" Nick exclaimed.

Everett quickly defended her. "Naw, man, not Jaime. She's one of the good ones, bruh."

"What makes you think that?" Dad questioned.

"I just keep getting this feeling that something isn't right. I can't describe it, but something just isn't quite kosher with her."

"But, why?" Nick asked.

"It's her actions. Ever since this whole Candy thing surfaced, she's been off her rocker. And it started with the bleach and knife episode. Her mood swings are worse than a woman on her period. She's drinking and doesn't think I know about it, and she's having these disappearing acts with no real explanation of where she's been."

My dad chimed in. "Slow down, Alonzo. You've said a mouthful. Let's just break this down bit by bit. Her reaction to the letter and her mood swings are pretty normal for someone who has been hurt. Women lash out all the time. That isn't unusual. Jaime being moody is also common. So, those two things don't add up to cheating. To me, her actions are pretty much typical for a woman who has been betrayed. Now, tell me more about the drinking."

"Well, she rarely drank before. A drink here and there. Now I'm finding empty wine glasses on her nightstand when I come home from work. Her side of the bed reeks of wine, and my faithful stash of alcohol is dwindling."

"Sounds like a woman trying to wash her troubles away with alcohol, bruh," Everett justified. "Still doesn't equate to infidelity to me."

I was getting a bit perturbed at how they continued to give good reason for Jaime's behavior. "Okay, well, explain her going out one night a little before midnight and not coming home until after two in the morning."

"Where did she say she had gone?" Dad asked.

"She claimed she was riding around to clear her head. It was the night she got the e-mail from Candy with the picture attached."

"Okay, that sounds a little suspicious, but had London received a picture of me like that, I would've preferred she take a drive to cool off," Nick commented. "Sometimes it's best to remove yourself from a situation if you think it may become volatile. Maybe she didn't want to pick up another knife, so instead she took a drive across the bridge to Maryland then turned around and came back."

I chuckled. "Whatever, man. Y'all are ride or die for her."

"No, it's not that at all," Nick stated. "It's just that I think you may be a little sensitive to her actions because of what you've done in the past. You're scared that she's going to repay you for all you've done to her."

Dad interjected, "It's called projection. It's a psychological term. Basically, it's a defense mechanism that involves taking one's own unacceptable qualities or feelings and ascribing them to other people. Basically, you haven't dealt with your own personal issues and the war going on inside you for your actions. Now, because of your indiscretions, you're placing those same behaviors on Jaime."

My dad made a good point. Maybe I was just overacting, but I still couldn't shake the feeling that something more was going on with Jaime. "So, y'all do agree that what she did the other night was out of order, right?"

"Oh, definitely," Everett affirmed.

"Yes, sir, that was out of order," Nick said, while my dad nodded in agreement.

"No excuse for her leaving home, staying out all night, and not telling a soul where she was. But that still doesn't mean she's having an affair," Everett stated.

"Look, son. You could worry yourself crazy about what Jaime is doing. Don't lose sleep over it. Believe me. Just like your involvement with Candy came to light, anything Jaime is doing will be exposed too."

"I don't mean to change the subject, y'all." Nick giggled. "But what's the latest with that chick, Candy? Man, she's a nutcase."

Before I could speak, my dad was all over it. "I called her supervisor right after that e-mail stunt. The same way she's trying to sabotage Alonzo's marriage and career, I'm gonna do to her. This tramp crossed the line when she started attacking the Clarke family."

Nick, Everett, and I just grinned as Dad talked about Candy. He was more passionate than I about making her pay for her cruel tricks, and I was going to let him have at it.

"So, is there any advice y'all can give a brother?" I asked. "'Cause, seriously, the last few weeks have been hell. And I'm sick of trying. I really am."

"Don't you say that, son. This is tough love talking now. You created this mess, so now you've got to stay the course until it gets better. You didn't give Jaime a choice of whether she wanted her heart shattered, so you can't determine when she puts the pieces of her heart back together. Sadly, you just gotta grin and bear it."

"I know it's tough, Alonzo," Nick sympathized. "But hang in there. This time next year it will all be a memory. You, Jaime, and Isaiah will be a happy family again. It's not going to be easy, nor will it be without its rough moments, but you'll get through it."

Everett offered his advice. "I'm with your dad and Nick. Don't turn your back on your family now. Until you can say you've done everything in your power to save your marriage, then you can't walk away. When things get a little combative at home, you've got us. We can plan to have more outings like this just to keep you sane. We're family. We got your back in this. Just don't give up—not now."

I was appreciative of their words of encouragement. Sometimes I wanted to give up because I felt like I was fighting a battle I couldn't win. If Jaime was never going to forgive me, then why should I have continued to try to appease her? My patience was growing thin, but I promised to heed the advice of my dad and friends and hang in there.

"I do have one more piece of advice," Dad said. "If that Candy woman contacts you, Jaime, or anyone connected to you one more time, slap a restraining order on her."

"Oh, Dad, my legal team and I already have some things brewing. Candy must've forgotten that I'm a lawyer. I can have her stopped. I just haven't taken aggressive measures at this point because I felt like I was somewhat deserving of it—like this was my payback for having an affair with a woman who is psychotic. But no more. If there is a next time, she will pay."

Chapter 29

"Hey, Jaime. Are you ready for me to try out my pho-tography skills?"

I was at Mario's apartment. Our digital photography class had ended. The drama in my life had impacted my learning, but Mario managed to learn a great deal. So he asked if I could be his subject to test just how much knowledge he gained.

"Yes, I'm ready." I was actually really excited.

Mario pulled out a gift bag and gave it to me.

"What's this?"

"Open it." He smiled.

Inside the gift bag was a black lace cut-out halter top teddy. "Oh, my goodness. This is sexy. I love it. Thank you." I gave him a big hug.

"Can you wear it for the pictures?"

"Sure. I'll be right back. I'll go change."

A few minutes later, I walked out of the bathroom wearing the seductive lingerie. I felt my body come alive wearing such a gorgeous teddy.

Mario whistled. "You look hot. I might not make it through the photo shoot."

"Well, if you do a good job, you might just get a treat afterward," I said, rubbing my love triangle.

I crawled onto Mario's bed. There, I posed in every position imaginable, at Mario's direction. This was ac-tually pretty fun for me. It was something new, some-thing exciting.

After Mario finished snapping pictures, he said, "I can't take it anymore." He climbed on top of me, kissing and undressing me at the same time. The foreplay was hot and heavy until my cell phone rang.

"Ignore it," Mario panted.

I did, as I too was enjoying the moment. My phone rang again. I disregarded it a second time. But the caller was persistent. Each time the person called and I didn't answer, he or she would hang up and dial again. This concerned me, and it took my focus from what Mario was doing to my body.

Finally, after several rings, I said, "Stop. Someone may be calling about my son." I got up, to Mario's displeasure, and answered my cell phone. It was Alonzo. "Shh. It's Alonzo," I mouthed.

"Hello?" I answered.

"Where are you?" Alonzo's tone was extremely irritated.

"At the mall?" I was shaken. Here I was standing damn near naked in Mario's apartment, talking to my husband, who was undoubtedly upset about something.

"I need you to come home now," he beckoned.

"Why?" I was nervous as hell, but delicate in my questioning.

"Just come home. It's urgent." He hung up.

"I gotta go," I blurted to Mario. I grabbed my clothes and hurriedly threw them on—first my undergarments, then I stepped into my jeans and almost strangled myself pulling my bebe shirt over my head. "Something's wrong. Alonzo told me to come home. He says it's urgent."

With a little fright in his eyes, Mario asked, "You don't think he knows about us, do you?"

"I don't know, but I gotta go. E-mail me the pics when you get a chance. I'll call you if I can."

I rushed out of Mario's apartment to my car. I was a nervous wreck. What could've been so vital? So pressing? Did something happen to Isaiah? My mom? My dad? Did he find out about me and Mario? I had so many questions, but no answers. I was scared.

Within twenty-five minutes of receiving Alonzo's call, I turned onto my block. My heart stopped when I pulled into my driveway to find two police cars sitting in front of my house. Something must have been horribly wrong. I jumped out of the car and ran over to Alonzo, who was talking to one of the officers.

"Alonzo, what's going on?" I questioned, panicky.

He didn't answer me. Instead, he introduced me to the policemen. "Officers, this is my wife."

"Hello, ma'am," one of the officers said.

I was so confused that my manners escaped me. I didn't even speak back to the policeman. "Alonzo, why are the police here? What happened?"

"Jaime, I've got some bad news. I know you're gonna be upset, but know that I am taking this matter very seriously. That's why the police are here."

I was growing impatient with Alonzo. "What? What?" I yelled.

"Look around," he said as he pointed in the directions of all our neighbors' yards. "Do you see the signs on the lawns?"

When I'd first driven into our neighborhood, I hadn't even noticed the sea of yard signs stuck in our neighbors' lawns. The signs resembled those election yard signs that people stuck in their grass to show support of their favorite candidate.

"What's wrong with the signs?" I asked.

Alonzo walked over and picked one up from the ground. He walked over to me and growled, "This one was stuck in our yard."

When he showed it to me, I could feel the blood within me begin to simmer. It wouldn't be long before I exploded. The sign had a picture of Alonzo and Candice posing together, with cheerful faces, and the words "you are my soul mate forever" written across the bottom of the sign.

"Let me guess, Candy put these in all our neighbors' yards, right?"

"Yes, Jaime," he responded with an apologetic facial expression.

I rolled my eyes and stormed into the house. A few minutes later, Alonzo entered the house. "Babe, I know you're upset. I am too. Enough is enough. Just so you know, I'm not taking this lightly. I'm taking legal action immediately. I promise you, this will be the last time she'll do something like this to disrupt our family."

I looked at Alonzo with doubt. "There's no way you can guarantee there won't be a next time. She just doesn't stop. Thongs, e-mails, flowers, and now yard signs. I mean, I can't deal with it." I began to feel weak. I walked over to the sofa to lie down.

"Jaime, are you feeling okay? You don't look good."

"I don't have the strength to fight this anymore, Alonzo. I just want to give up. I want her to win, so she will stop. It's one thing for us to have to endure this treatment, but she involved your coworkers, our family, friends, and now our neighbors. I'm done fighting this battle. I won't do it anymore."

"You don't have to fight. I'm fighting for you—for us. Just sit back and watch how I defeat the enemy."

I just lay there, not saying a word. I felt faint and my stomach ached. This was all too much for me.

"Jaime, say something, please," Alonzo pleaded.

"There's nothing left to say besides I'm unhappy. I'm sick. I'm hurt. And now that my neighbors are all in my business, I'm embarrassed."

"I'm sorry. I can't apologize enough for all of this. But I'm gonna make it better. Just watch and see."

Alonzo picked me up from the sofa and carried me upstairs to the bedroom. He laid me on the bed and placed a blanket over me. He then lay on the opposite side on the bed and said, "Can you please tell me about your illness? I really want to know how I can help you. Right now, you seem really out of it, and I'm not sure how much of it is because of the yard signs or because you're sick. Please talk to me. I wanna help." His pleas seemed sincere, and because of that, I opened up to him.

For the next hour, Alonzo and I talked about Crohn's disease—the cause, symptoms, and treatments. He was really attentive and inquired a lot as to how he could help. When I told him about stress, an expression of sadness overcame him. "I know I'm the main source of your stress, but I promise this will change. This will change."

I informed him that I was given two prescriptions that I hadn't filled yet, and he offered to have them filled immediately. Alonzo also made a list of a few of my favorite treats to pick up while he was out at the store.

While he was gone, I lay in bed with my eyes closed. For the first time in weeks, I felt a sense of peace. I had no idea why, but I also noticed that while I was talking to Alonzo about my ailment, we seemed to connect in ways that we hadn't in a long time. It felt good to have a decent conversation with him. It felt good to talk to him without feeling bitter or spewing venom. It felt good to lie beside him in bed and not feel repulsed.

The whole day had been one big, twisted mess. I went from posing on Mario's bed in lingerie, to seeing yard signs of my husband with another woman, to feeling a bond with Alonzo that I hadn't felt in a long time. What sane person does that? My daily actions or reactions to events weren't normal. I was no longer a rational thinker. I no longer exhibited morals. I no longer displayed the strength of a strong black woman. I had given up the fight. I was down for whatever, whenever. And to top it off, I still wanted to drink even after my diagnosis.

If I'd never wanted to admit it before, I realized now that my mom, London, and Riah were correct. I needed psychological help—fast.

Chapter 30

I awakened this morning with the conversation between Alonzo and me still replaying in my mind. I was also baffled about how I didn't allow feelings of anger to linger following Candy's latest stunt. Although I was extremely embarrassed by what she had done, I didn't lash out at Alonzo like I had done so many times in the past. I guess part of me just didn't want to fight anymore. I didn't have the strength to do it, but, beyond that, something about my reaction to the situation was different, and I couldn't identify the reason.

I also thought I'd heard sincerity in Alonzo's voice when he and I had our heart-to-heart talk about my chronic illness. I felt like he actually cared about me. However, as much as I wanted to believe that, I was too afraid to give in to those feelings. I didn't want to let my guard down with Alonzo just yet. I couldn't risk my heart being hurt by him anymore. I wanted to talk to someone about it, so I called Riah. I asked her to meet me for brunch. I chose Riah and not both she and London because I also planned to tell Riah about my affair with Mario. Between the two, I thought Riah would be less likely to share my clandestine lifestyle with anyone in my family. I trusted London, but I didn't want to risk her accidentally letting my secrets slip to her mom, who would surely tell my mom.

"Good morning, Riah." I greeted her with a hug and a kiss on her cheek.

"Good morning, darling," she said cheerfully.

I had chosen to dine at the Fireside Grill because we both loved their brunch buffet. We didn't waste any time piling food on our plates to stuff our bellies.

"You don't have anything spicy on your plate, do you?" Riah asked, eyeing my plate.

"*No*, Riah. Dang. I don't want my stomach to burn any more than you do. I'm not gonna eat anything I'm not supposed to."

She playfully rolled her eyes. "Just keeping you in check."

After a few bites to eat, Riah said, "So what's up? You said you wanted to talk about something. I'm all ears."

"Okay. First, I need you to promise me that this conversation goes no further than the two of us. You can't tell a soul. Not Everett. Not London. Not the dog. Nobody. You must die with this information."

She frowned. "Damn. Is it that serious?"

"Yeah, I'm afraid it is."

"Yes, Jaime, you have my word. What you say to me is between the two of us. As long as we've been friends, you know I've never betrayed your trust, and I won't start now."

"That's why I love you." I smiled. "Anyway, first let me tell you that something happened yesterday. This is not the top-secret stuff, but I wanted to get your thoughts on it."

"Okay." Riah was listening attentively.

"This morning when we talked, I told you about the signs Candy put in my yard and my neighbors' yards."

"Hmph. Ol' trifling heifer. That whore needs to be stomped, for real."

"I know. I know. It's way overdue. Anyway, after that incident, I came in the house. I was exhausted. Just mentally drained, tired of it all. I felt faint. Went to lie down on the couch. Alonzo came in really concerned. He carried me upstairs, covered me with a blanket, and lay beside me and just wanted to talk."

"About what? That hooker?" Riah snapped.

"Nope. About me: my health and how he could help me. He wanted to know what he could do to help me cope with the illness. His words were gentle. He seemed sincere and attentive to my needs."

"Well, that's wonderful. I'm glad to hear that."

"I *know*. I was like, is this my husband? I hadn't seen that caring, tender side in a long time. I liked it. I actually liked him for the moment. I wasn't even as concerned about the Candy fiasco after that. But then . . ."

"But then what?"

"I found myself afraid to give into him. It's Alonzo we're talking about. He's the ultimate smooth operator. He knows what to say and how to say it. He has the gift of gab. I wondered if he was really genuine or was he just playing a role with me last night."

"You can't do that to yourself, Jaime. You can't. Initially, I wanted you to leave him. But after Everett told me how much effort Alonzo's putting into fixing his family, I respect him for that. Believe it or not, he's made changes. Whether you want to see them or not, he has. Example number one: he's home more now than ever before. That's huge for him."

"I agree. He's made some changes, but I've been too caught up in my 'woe is me' pity party to see it."

"Well, open your eyes, girlfriend. I think what you experienced last night with Alonzo was a good thing. It was the step in the right direction. Sounds to me like you're more receptive to forgiving him."

I shook my head. "I don't know about that."

"What do you mean?"

"Well, that's because you don't know everything. This is the part where you can never tell a soul."

"I already told you I wouldn't. Now what?" Riah's tone was impatient.

I looked down at my plate of food. I was a little on edge about admitting this to anyone, but in order to get a true assessment about my marriage, I needed to tell Riah the whole story. I sighed. She looked at me like she wanted to choke the words out of my mouth.

"Riah." I spoke softly. "I'm a sinner."

She laughed. "Aren't we all?"

"No. Not like this. This one is really bad."

"Um, no. In God's eyes, no sin is greater than the other."

"Well, in my eyes this is really bad, and I'm not sure God or Alonzo will forgive me."

"Oh, Jaime, stop being silly. God will forgive you if you *truly* repent. As for Alonzo, he can't begin to judge. He had his own list of sins to repent for. So, what's the big deal? Did you steal something? Did you kill some-body? Did you commit adultery? What?"

"The last," I whispered.

"Huh? I can't hear you."

I spoke louder. "The last one you said."

Immediate sadness was shown in Riah's eyes. I'd known that she wouldn't approve, but I knew she wouldn't be too harsh with me because of it.

"Aw, Jaime. Really? You've been cheatin' on Alonzo?"

"Yeah," I responded sadly.

"Why?"

"Because I gave up. I gave up hope on our mar-riage, that he'd ever love me and be faithful to me. So I stopped trying to fulfill my duties as his wife and found myself involved in a relationship outside my marriage."

"Who is it?"

"This guy from the class I was taking."

"Do you love him?"

"Hell, no. I don't even want to be with him like that. He was just someone to make me feel good and up-lifted because Alonzo didn't anymore. He showed me he cared. He told me I was beautiful. He made me feel special. Let's just say, all the things Alonzo should've been saying and doing as my husband, this guy did it."

"Are you still seeing him?"

"I was, but after last night with Alonzo, I don't know what to do. That's why I asked to meet with you."

"So, are you ready for my opinion? My honest opin-ion?"

"Yeah, girl. Give it to me."

"I want you to end this affair. I believe this thing you've got going on outside your marriage is what's blocking you from fully reconciling with Alonzo. I think you keep throwing up Alonzo's indiscretions as excuses for you to keep seeing this guy. You're using Alonzo's actions to justify your behavior. That's not right, and it makes you no better than him. Next, you can't con-tinue to berate your husband for cheating on you when you're doing the same. If that ain't the pot calling the kettle black . . ."

"But, Riah, he's done it to me forever. I've only done it once," I lied. There was no way I'd ever tell her about the bathroom incident. No way, no how.

"Doesn't matter. Two wrongs don't make a right, and I don't wanna hear nothin' about making it even. That's all bull crap. And the last thing is this: you know God. You may not have a church home right now, and you may not feel like you can trust a pastor at the mo-ment, but no matter what, God is in your heart. Your Heavenly Father is weeping over this behavior, and you know it. You've got to do better, Jaime."

Riah was making me feel bad. Still, I didn't feel judged, but that she was telling the truth and not just what I wanted to hear, like a friend should.

"I love you like my sister, Jaime, and I want better for you than this. I don't want you to be caught up in some scandalous affair with some dude who really doesn't care about you. Yeah, he may seem all nice, sweet, and kind, but for real, you know the deal with this man."

"I know. You've given me a lot to think about."

"I hope so. You need to call it quits with this penis-on-the-side now. Don't wait another few days or weeks. It needs to stop immediately. You connected with your husband last night. That's where you need to be. Focus your attention there, and if your marriage fails, and it's really meant for you and this guy to be together, then he'll be waiting for you with open arms—once you're no longer married. Until then, he's got to go."

"Thanks, Riah. I appreciate your honesty. Are you mad at me?"

"Girl, no. I'm just glad I finally know what's going on. I knew something was different about you. I knew it was more than Pastor Steele, Alonzo, and Crohn's disease. I never guessed you were leading a double life, but I knew something wasn't right about my friend. Honey, I ain't perfect. I can't judge you or the next person. I have my flaws. But I love you too much not to be honest with you. This affair isn't a good idea. Drop that Negro—now."

Riah and I finished our brunch and then went for a nice walk. It felt good to finally disclose to someone my relationship with Mario. It was hard keeping it bottled up. I agreed with Riah that I needed to break things off with Mario. It was time to get my life back on track and at least give Alonzo and my marriage another chance. But before I officially ended things with Mario, I had to have one more tryst.

Chapter 31

Spring break had arrived and Isaiah had been out of school all week. Punishment seemed to have served him well, as his third quarter report card showed improvement in all of his classes. He still didn't make the honor roll and was achieving below the A student we had been accustomed to, but I praised him for making small steps toward improvement.

During his vacation from school, Isaiah spent quality time bonding with his family. He and I traveled into DC to visit the International Spy Museum, Madame Tussauds, and the Smithsonian's National Museum of Natural History's IMAX Theater. We had a great time—just the two of us. He also attended a Washington Nationals baseball game with his dad, and both of his grandfathers had taken him to a Washington Wizards game where he said he had a blast hanging out with the elder men in his life.

Alonzo and I had paid for Isaiah to travel to Baltimore on the Friday of his spring break, to participate in a two-day youth program called Challenge Discovery. Because of all the trouble Isaiah had gotten into in recent months, we were hesitant to allow him to attend, but his basketball coach begged us to allow him to be a part of this program. The coach stressed how great Challenge Discovery was in focusing on team building, personal awareness, developing individual self-esteem, and empowerment. He also stated that the

program helped to emphasize interpersonal relationships. After discussing at length whether Isaiah should
attend, Alonzo and I decided it would be a good idea.
The entire basketball team would be a part of this experience, and we could only see positive things arise
from Isaiah and his peers participating. Along with
the coach, the assistant coach and several other school
staff would be traveling with the team, so they would
be well chaperoned.

Isaiah was excited about this venture. He had been
confined to the house for weeks, so this was his first
taste of freedom.

"Isaiah, did you make sure to pack your toothbrush,
toothpaste, pajamas, towel, wash—"

"Ma," Isaiah interrupted me. "I have everything packed.
We've looked over my bag ten times. I haven't forgotten
anything. And if I have, I'll just use some of the spending
money you and dad gave me."

"Okay, Isaiah. I guess that's your way of telling me to
stop treating you like a baby, huh?"

"Yeah. I'm good."

"Just make sure you secure that money we gave you.
We're sending you off with a nice chunk of change.
Don't lose it, and don't leave it lying around. You don't
want your roommate to steal it."

Isaiah just shook his head. I could tell he was tired of
hearing my overprotective speeches. But I wasn't done
yet.

"Now, when you walk out this door, you make sure
you listen to your coach and all the staff. I don't want
any bad reports, Isaiah, or you'll never attend anything
like this again. You're still punished, you know? The
only reason you're going on this trip is because your
coach begged us to allow you to participate. So, you
better behave, be respectful, and take away something
positive from this experience."

"All right, Ma. I'll be on my best behavior. No bad reports." He walked over to hug me.

"Don't be trying to hug all on me to get me to stop lecturing you. I still have a few more rules to give you."

"Oops, sorry, Ma. The bus is here." Just as I was about to give Isaiah more laws of the land, a white shuttle bus pulled in front of our house. Isaiah was elated. "Saved by the coach," he teased.

As I walked Isaiah out to the bus, I said, "I love you. Be safe, be careful, be good, and call me when you arrive."

"Will do all of the above, Mom."

He climbed on to the bus to greet his team. I spoke briefly with Coach Walker, who handed me a sheet of paper with the hotel information and all the contact information for each of the staff members. He also gave me an itinerary for the weekend, which included two days at Challenge Discovery and returning home on Sunday afternoon. I said my last good-bye, reminded him to call me, and waved as the bus drove away.

Excitedly, I clicked my heels together, because I had the house to myself. It was Friday, Isaiah was gone, Alonzo was working late, and I had to prepare for my night. This would be my last rendezvous with Mario. I was ending the affair, but I wanted to end this salacious part of my life with a bang.

Mario had gotten an invite to attend a "special" party, and he'd asked me to go with him. Initially, I declined, but after some thought I gave in to his request because I knew our relationship was ending. As terrified as I was to attend, my finale with Mario would be attending a swingers' party in the nation's capital. This was extremely out of character for me, but I felt I owed Mario something for being so caring, friendly, uplifting, and accommodating to me. It was the least I could do to say thank you just before I said good-bye forever.

***

It took me two hours to get ready for the evening. The entire time, I was nervous. This was a new experience for me. I would've never guessed in a million years that I, Jaime Clarke, would be attending a swingers' party. I always thought the lifestyle was immoral. I thought sex should be between two people in a monogamous relationship. When having discussions about swingers in the past, I described them as dirty people who didn't use protection. I used to turn my nose up at the thought of anyone swapping bodily fluids with a stadium full of strangers. The whole idea of swinging was just gross, made my stomach turn. I never could've imagined considering being a part of something like this, but I agreed. And not only was I attending, I was starting to get a little excited about this venture.

Prior to the party, Mario sent the personal invitation to me via e-mail. It stated that the party started at 7:00 P.M., but Mario and I were not planning to arrive until 8:00 P.M. I left before Alonzo arrived home from work. I called him to tell him that I didn't want to sit in the house alone and wanted to go out for some fresh air, to the mall to do some shopping and catch a movie. I figured that would buy me some time if he questioned my whereabouts. I didn't plan to stay out too long. I packed a small bag with a change of clothing: jeans, a DKNY T-shirt, and sneakers. I planned to change outfits just in case Alonzo happened to arrive home before I did. He'd have my head on a platter if I walked through the door dressed in grown and sexy attire when I was supposedly shopping at the mall and going to a movie theater.

As I drove to a parking garage in Roslyn, Virginia, the destination where Mario and I had planned to meet, I thought about this being my last time with him. I hadn't

wavered from my decision to work on my marriage, but
I just wanted to get this last bit of bad girl out of my system. I didn't know how I was going to tell Mario, but I
hoped that we could part amicably. He was really a nice
guy, and I would have hated for things to end messily
between us.

Shortly after I'd pulled into my parking space, Mario
arrived. He was dressed in a white collared shirt with
blue jeans and dress shoes. He looked really nice and
smelled delicious.

"Hi, Jaime." He flashed a wide grin. "You look sexy
as hell, girl."

"Thanks." I blushed. *I guess all that primping paid
off.* I had gone through ten outfits before I decided to
wear a black one-shoulder bubble dress and silver sti-
letto heels. There was a chill in April's night air, and I
was a tad bit chilly, but I looked cute. "You're looking
mighty handsome yourself," I said as he opened his
passenger door for me.

"So, are you ready?" Mario asked before closing the
door.

"I guess so," I answered, and then sighed.

As Mario drove to the mansion for the party, he
began to explain the rules to me. I was extremely overwhelmed by all the information he unloaded. "Here's
the deal. There are various types of swinging. There is
soft swap, full swap, or group swap."

I frowned. "What the hell is soft swap, full swap, and
all that stuff?"

Mario laughed. "Okay, quick answers: Soft swap is
no penetration, just oral sex. Full swap is penetrative
sex. Group swap is self-explanatory. We need to come
up with our rules before we get there. Because this is
your first time, I want you to feel as comfortable as
possible. We won't do anything you don't want to do."

Honestly, after those explanations, I didn't want to do any of it. But I didn't want to be a party pooper. I responded, "I don't want oral sex, and I don't want same sex stuff, so maybe I'll just do penetrative sex. I guess that's full swap. You with a girl and me with a dude."

"That's fine. Now, do we want another couple or singles?"

"Damn, Mario. Why is this so involved?" I frowned. Why did this lifestyle have to be so difficult? It was just sex.

"You silly, girl. There are a lot more rules than I'm giving you right now, but I don't want to overwhelm you since this is a cram session. We probably should've talked about this in detail sooner."

"Ya think? Anyway, I don't want to mess around with other couples. Why the hell are they there, anyway? I mean, if you're married, you should be sexing your husband and wife at home, not sharing them with someone else publicly."

"That's your view on it, Jaime. Some say swinging has saved their marriage and it's better than cheating."

"Whatever. I ain't buying. But, anyway, only singles. I don't want some woman getting mad at me when her husband gets a feel of my good-good and may decide to leave her," I teased.

"Out-of-control," Mario remarked. "I want you to loosen up. When you get there, mingle and get a few drinks. We don't have to hook up right away."

"Do we have to hook up with multiple people? Can you just do one girl, and I do one guy, and that's it?"

Mario reached over and rubbed the back of my head. "We'll do whatever makes you comfortable."

"Thanks, babe."

When Mario and I arrived at our destination, he parked the car on the street. The butterflies in my stomach were having a party of their own. I was so on edge that I really wanted to tell Mario that I'd wait in the car, but I decided against it. This was supposed to be my last wild, fun, and crazy night, and I wanted to follow through with my plans. Arm in arm, we began walking up the driveway to the mansion's doorstep. Music and disco lights emanated from the house, and scantily clad individuals passed by the floor-to-ceiling windows. A few people lingered on the patio, probably nervous like me. Once inside, I was glued to Mario as he searched for the hostess named Passion, the woman who had invited him to the party. He couldn't find her, so we made a mad dash to the food spread and bar. As we maneuvered throughout the mansion, I was in awe by what I saw. I had never laid eyes upon anything of this nature. As described in the invitation, the house was immaculate. The basement was decked out with curtains that sectioned off plush mattresses and pillows. The lavish seclusions beckoned the next kinky group, but all I could think about was what was left on the beds from the group before. Another room had an elaborate sex swing anchored to the ceiling, with mattresses surrounding it like pews around a pulpit. Porn flashed on a big-screen TV, a stripper pole stood erect on the dance floor, and pool sharks played with their sticks and balls.

I stood so closely to Mario you would've thought we were joined at the hip. This environment was surreal. I gulped my drink and scanned the room to observe the people. The guests were all fairly attractive, normal-looking people, with ages ranging from late twenties to late forties. Many of the couples were scattered throughout the house, snuggling, dancing, and admiring from the sides just like we were. However, the singles mingled more with others. I couldn't believe a stripper contest took place as I watched from afar. But, for some strange reason, I couldn't tear my eyes away as the women tossed themselves around the pole, taking off more and more clothing as the song progressed. I almost died from laughter when a big, chunky woman with electric blue lingerie and knee-high hooker boots decided to throw her big self around the stripper pole and landed on the floor. I needed that laugh. It definitely loosened me up a bit. Eventually, the dance floor cleared as couples and groups moseyed off to finish what they had come for. Naked coed gatherings were now in full swing behind the velvet curtains. A couple started walking in the direction of Mario and me. Immediately, I became anxious. I knew this guy was about to approach me for sex because he had been giving me the eye across the room for the last thirty minutes. I'd thought he was alone, but I saw now that he had a woman following him. "Good evening," the gentleman said.

"Hi," Mario said, extending his hand.

"Would you and your lady like to go upstairs with me and my girlfriend to chat?"

Before Mario could respond, I quickly answered, "No, thank you."

The man gave a slight smile and walked away with his woman. Mario chuckled and shook his head at me. "What was wrong with them?"

"First, they are a couple. Girlfriend and boyfriend equals a relationship—a couple. Secondly, he wasn't cute."

While I stood in the same spot like the wallflower Mario asked me not to be, a woman approached us. She was a light brown woman with long blond hair and huge breasts. When she reached us, her boobs met us first. "Hey. My girlfriend and I were looking at you from across the room. Would you like to go to one of the rooms and get to know each other better?" she asked cheerfully.

Mario's face was with bright with enthusiasm. I could tell he wanted to go. He spied her friend from across the room, and she was just as bodacious, blond, and bubbly. But I quickly shut down the idea.

"I'm sorry. I'm a newbie at this, and I'm still trying to get comfortable. Can you just give me some more time, and we'll catch up with you later?"

"No problem, honey," she said as she flipped her hair. "I was once new too. I understand."

As she bounced away, Mario couldn't take his eyes off her round bottom. I slapped his arm to get his attention. "Mario."

"What?" He jumped. Then he joked, "Why did you turn her away? I was interested in a full swap with her."

"*Mario*. First of all, her friend was a girl. I said I wasn't gonna hook up with no girl."

"Jaime, they could've both had me," he stated.

"Oh, really?" I said with a hint of jealousy. I knew at that moment it was time to go. I had never in my life felt comfortable with sharing my man; not my boyfriend, fiancé, husband, or even my little boy toy on the side. As much as I wanted to end my affair with Mario with a bang, attending the "Spring Fling" swingers' party just wasn't me. I couldn't do it.

I locked arms with Mario and said, "I hate to ruin your fun, but I don't think I can do this anymore. This isn't my crowd."

Mario wrapped his arms around my neck and said, "It's understandable. You're not ruining my fun. Just spending time with you has been great. I always have fun, no matter what we do."

Once we agreed there would be no swinging for us, we left the party, walked down the long driveway, and got in the car. Because I had successfully messed up the evening, I decided not to tell Mario at that moment that I couldn't see him anymore. I would wait a couple of days, and then break the news to him. My delay didn't mean that I had changed my mind about ending the relationship. I just wanted to be gentle in my approach, and I didn't think this was the right time to do it.

At 11:00 P.M., Mario took me back to my car, where I took out the extra set of clothing I had stored in the trunk. I hurriedly changed in the back seat.

Thank goodness my "cover your tracks" instincts kicked in with the change of clothing. Alonzo would be oblivious to the fact that I had actually been dressed in sexy attire, attending a swingers' party.

Chapter 32

When I arrived home, Alonzo's car was parked in the driveway. There was a light coming from the living room, which was a bit odd. He was usually in the bedroom or in the family room, watching television after a long, hard day at work. I already had my story together in case he asked me why I was coming home after midnight from shopping and a movie. I had a shopping bag in the car with articles of clothing that I planned to return to the store. I grabbed it so I would have something to show from my "shopping spree." But I didn't have a ticket stub from the movies. I'd just tell him I lost it or threw it away.

Why am I stressing so much? I really didn't owe Alonzo any explanations. Hell, his only ultimatum to me was to not stay out all night again or he'd be gone. I actually was arriving home early. So everything should've been fine.

With my faux shopping bag in hand, I walked up to the front door. As soon as I put my key in the door, it opened. "Hey, thanks for opening the door," I said as I walked directly past him. I was going to head straight upstairs so I didn't have to engage in conversation with him, but Alonzo wasn't letting me slip by so easily.

"So, you're a swinger now?" he spat with a look of disgust.

I was totally caught by surprise. I didn't know how to respond. "Huh?"

"I said you're a swinger now?"

I grimaced. "What are you talking about? No, I'm not."

"Don't fuckin' lie to me, Jaime," he bellowed with fury.

"I'm not lying to you. I know nothing about swinging." I knew I must've had the word *"Busted"* written in all capital letters across my forehead. I really didn't know how to react to Alonzo's questioning. *How in the world did he find out? And how do I explain myself out of this one?*

Alonzo walked over to me and said, "Jaime, I'm an attorney in Washington, DC. I'm well connected. I know plenty of people. I also know a lot of folks who wear business suits and ties during the day, but are freaky at night. One of those folks who happen to like wild, kinky orgies coincidentally was at a mansion tonight at Georgetown."

I gasped. I didn't know how to respond to Alonzo. I just stood in the middle of the floor, looking at Alonzo break down how I was totally caught in the act.

"See, when I paraded you around town to all those galas, dinners, and office holiday parties, people got to know you," he continued. "People know your face. They've seen you not only in public, but repeatedly as they walk into my office and see your picture sitting on my desk. So, you can imagine my surprise when one of the folks I know saw you at a party with a man who wasn't me. He was quite shocked to see your face in the mansion. So he sent a picture message to my cell phone that said, 'Is this your wife?'"

Alonzo paused. He walked over to the living room table and picked up his cell. He then walked over to me and showed me the picture of me wearing my sexy black dress, standing arm in arm with Mario and a

drink in my other hand. There was no denying it was
me, but what baffled me more was the fact that these
swingers' parties were supposed to not allow people
to take pictures because they claimed to value privacy.
Someone had violated the rules.

In a sarcastic tone, Alonzo asked, "So is that you,
Jaime, with another man?"

I didn't answer. Growing impatient by my silence,
Alonzo quickly grabbed me by the throat and said,
"Answer me!"

I struggled to breath. I tried to pry Alonzo's fingers
from around my neck, but to no avail. The more I
pulled at his fingers, the tighter his grip became.

"So you're a whore now? A cheating whore? You're
not just cheating, but you're swinging, too," he barked,
as he continued his attempt to strangle me.

I made many efforts to fight back, but Alonzo's grip
was too tight, and my oxygen was decreasing. I couldn't
believe that he was actually going to choke me to death.
Then he let me go with a violent push. I fell to the floor,
coughing uncontrollably, rubbing my neck, trying to
catch my breath. While I was on the floor, Alonzo continued to spew his venom.

"So, you're fucking Mario Fox, huh? That's your twenty-
five-year-old boyfriend?" he questioned angrily.

I didn't answer.

"Ya see, after I got that picture message, I decided to
do a little research. However, I didn't have to look very
hard. I happened to go to the computer room and see
that your e-mail was still open after checking out the
invitation to the swingers' party. Surprisingly, not only
did I see the Spring Fling invite, but I also saw pictures
taken of you in lingerie, posing seductively. Ya never
did that shit for me. So Mario got you wide open like

that—he can get you to wear sexy shit and high heels and lie spread eagle on his bed? Now he got you swapping sex with multiple strangers. So tell me. How does it feel to be a slut?"

Alonzo's rant was never-ending. Finally, after overcoming the choking episode and sitting on the floor listening to him berate me, I had had enough. I looked up at him and screamed, "Shut the fuck up! You don't know what you're talkin' about. Yes, I was at the party, but I didn't have sex with anybody. It wasn't my type of party."

"Ha." Alonzo gave a sarcastic chuckle. "Tell that bull to somebody who will believe it, 'cause I don't."

"I don't care what you believe. I know what I did and didn't do. I attended the party, but I didn't have sex. And, yes, I have been with Mario. It's wrong, but it just happened. There was nothing planned about us being together. It was a friendship that formed out of vulnerability, grief, and hopelessness. I had given up on you and on us. I got tired of you making me feel like shit. All you ever did in this relationship was walk all over me. You disrespected me time and time again, and I finally got tired of the bullshit. I sacrificed my life for you, raised our son alone, and you repaid me by treating me like shit. You don't respect me, you emotionally abuse me, and after so many years of your emotional turmoil, I said fuck it. I threw in the towel. I wanted to leave, but I couldn't. I don't have anything. No education, no money, no self-esteem, no nothing. So I did the next best thing, and that was to find somebody who could help me take my mind off of you and all the hell you've put me through. That's what Mario did for me."

A sudden burst of energy had overcome me. I slowly got up from the floor, stood tall, and looked Alonzo dead in the eyes. This time I was ready for a fight. I was tired of being in this tortuous relationship, and if tonight was going to be the end of our marriage, then I was going to give him just a small piece of the hell he had given me for so many years.

Alonzo was still irate, but I didn't give a flying flip. He was going to feel every ounce of venom I had to spew at this very moment. "How dare you call me a whore? You have some fuckin' nerve. You're the man whore! We can't even begin to count the number of women you've been with, so don't even form your lips to ever call me a slut or a whore. You've had multiple affairs. I've had two."

"Two?" Alonzo shrieked.

"Yes, dammit, two. One was a lapse in judgment, a one-night stand that happened out of anger after seeing that picture of you in bondage in Candy's bed. The other was with Mario. That's it," I said, hoping my admission would make his world crumble. He needed to feel the excruciating pain that I'd endured repeatedly after learning about his affairs.

I continued, "The one-night stand I've never seen again. But Mario . . . Mario was there for me during a time when I was hurting emotionally and physically. He showed me he cared. He listened. He let me cry. He didn't judge me. He never thought he was better than me. He told me I was beautiful and smart. Hell, he did just about everything that you don't do."

I paused briefly to catch my breath. "I'll admit it. Yes, I bonded with Mario. Yes, I took sexy pictures. But am I a swinger? Hell no! And I don't give a damn if you believe me or not. What you accept as truth doesn't matter to me anymore. And if the fact that I had a relationship with Mario affects your manhood that deeply, then leave. Feel free to draw up some papers. Let's separate, divorce, but whatever you do, just let me be free. You don't wanna be here anyway. The only reason we're together now is out of obligation."

Alonzo retorted, "That's not true, and you know it!"

"Oh, yes, the hell it is. If it had not been for Isaiah, you would've left me when you went to Atlanta, and never looked back. You married me because your mom died. One of her deathbed wishes was for you to marry me and make a home for me and Isaiah. You don't love me. You never have. So, do what you gotta do. I just don't care anymore. I don't want to fuss and fight. I don't want to live this uncomfortable lifestyle any longer. I'm not happy, you're not happy, so let's stop the games."

"I married you because I love you. It had nothing to do with my mom."

"Bull crap," I screamed. I was sick of his lies and this was yet another one.

"Look, Jaime, I know I've put you through hell, but nothing I've done justifies your actions. There's no excuse for hooking up with strangers for a one-night stand and this young dude, posing like you're in *Playboy* magazine, going to swingers' parties, and whatever else you've done. You got me messed up behind this."

I chuckled. "Funny, how you can dish the shit, but can't take it. As long as you are stomping all over my heart, it's gravy. But the minute the tables turn, you don't know what to do—you're messed up. Well, I'm giving you an out. I'm telling you, you have my permission to go live happily ever after with Candy Barr. Maybe you can choke her up a time or two after she finishes handcuffing you to the bed."

"Jaime, stop it! Just stop it."

"I will not stop. You don't get it, do you? You destroyed my soul. Love doesn't involve hurt, lies, and the destruction of someone's spirit. You've done all that to me. And just recently, after all of that, I was willing to give it another go. Tonight I had planned to end things with Mario. I was not going to be seeing him anymore. But then I come home to this self-righteous, my-shit-don't-stink husband who attempts to strangle me, and I realize none of this is worth it anymore. So, if this situation with Mario has sent you over the edge and bruised your ego to the point that you can't take it, I understand. Just bounce anytime you're ready."

"This is my house too, Jaime. Stop telling me to leave. I can't believe your attitude is this callous. I am disappointed in you, and hurt that you would engage in such activities, and all you can do is tell *me* to leave. Who do you think you are?"

"I'm tired. Aren't you? The past few months have been pure hell. It's time for some peace. I don't have the strength to deal with it all anymore. I don't have faith you'll change, and now you think I'm a whore, so why even fake it? That's all I'm saying."

"I know our problems are deep, and I've been trying to work on them, but you've just complicated things further with this mess. I expected so much more of you, Jaime."

"Whatever, Alonzo," I snapped. "I don't want to hear that shit. I expected more of you a long time ago. Cut the disappointment lecture. Save that for Isaiah."

"You're not the same person anymore. I don't know who you are, and I really can't stand the person you've become," Alonzo exclaimed.

"Well, then pat yourself on the back because you created this new Jaime."

"No, you cut the crap! I am not the blame for—"

The home telephone rang, interrupting Alonzo midsentence. It startled both of us. Here we were in the middle of a firestorm and the phone rang at 12:30 in the morning. Alonzo answered and my heart stopped as I listened. I knew this was not a good call, but I had no idea what it was in reference to. My ears were piqued when Alonzo said, "Okay. What happened? What hospital? We're on our way."

He slammed down the phone and said, "Jaime, we've got to get on the road to Baltimore. That was Isaiah's coach. There's been an accident, and Isaiah has been taken to shock trauma at University of Maryland Medical Center. We need to leave now."

"Shock trauma? Oh, my goodness. Is it bad?"

"I don't know all the details. Coach just urged us to get there immediately. Let's go," Alonzo said, grabbing his car keys.

With one ring of the telephone, the argument ceased. Was it completely over? I highly doubted that, but as of now we had to put our disdain for one another on the back burner and head to Baltimore to see about Isaiah.

"Please, God, cover my baby," I prayed as we ran out of the house.

Chapter 33

Although Alonzo and I were, without question, still miffed at each other, our anger was overshadowed by our concern for Isaiah. Within minutes of receiving the phone call from Isaiah's coach, we were speeding up 95 North toward Baltimore. Coach Walker had given Alonzo the hospital's name and address. While in the car, I called my parents to inform them of what happened.

"Hi, Dad. Sorry to wake you," I said, sobbing, "but Isaiah's in the hospital."

"Why? What happened?" my dad asked in a panic.

"I don't know all the details. His coach called around twelve-thirty this morning. Alonzo talked to him. All he said was that we needed to get to the hospital quickly because Isaiah had been transported to shock trauma. We're on the road now going to Baltimore."

"Your mother and I are on our way. Don't worry, sweetheart. Isaiah is going to be all right. Stay strong, and we'll see you shortly."

After I hung up with my dad, I sat in the passenger seat of Alonzo's truck and cried my eyes out. I was scared as hell, and I felt responsible. This was God unleashing his wrath upon me for my despicable behavior. Not only had I turned my back on Him, the church, and my husband, but I was in the streets acting like a damn fool, had been caught in an affair with a child ten years my junior, I was sexing strangers in the bathroom, drinking alcohol like it was water, and I'd also neglected my son. Now God was repaying me for all my sins. I couldn't do anything but cry and cry out to the Lord.

As I rocked back and forth, I cried out desperately to my Father in heaven. "Lord, please forgive me. I'm so sorry, Lord. I repent for all the things that I've done wrong. I repent for everything that I have said and done. I know my actions haven't been of you, Lord. I know my heart and mind haven't been on you, God, but *please, please* don't take my baby. I love him, Lord. I really do, and I promise if you save him, I'll do better. I'll be a better person. I'll go back to church. I'll worship you. I've give you all the glory and honor and praise. I'll live for you for eternity, Lord. I'll completely turn away from sin. Please, God. Please, please bring healing to my child, God."

For the entire ride, I rocked and wept, and whispered, "Please, God, cover him. Please, God, cover him." While I softy prayed, I heard Alonzo call his dad on his cell phone.

As he spoke, he sniffled. "Dad, it's me. I apologize for this early morning call, but I wanted to let you know that Isaiah is in the hospital. Yeah, Jaime and I are on our way to Baltimore now. We're about thirty minutes away. All we know is there was a fight and Isaiah was taken to the hospital. His coach called a little after midnight, and we hit the road immediately." Alonzo paused and sniffled again. "No, Dad, you don't have to come out. I can give you updates from the hospital. Okay, if you insist. If you get a pen and paper, I'll give you the address."

Just like my parents, Alonzo's dad was crazy about Isaiah. He was their only grandchild, and he was spoiled as heck. It was no surprise to me that both maternal and paternal grandparents got out of their beds to rush to Maryland to see about him. He was a special child, a gift from God, and we all loved him dearly.

When Alonzo hung up, he said, "My dad wants to meet us at the hospital. He said there's no way he'd be able to go back to sleep after getting that call. He said he'd rather be at the hospital than pacing back and forth in the house all morning."

"I'm glad. I'm sure Isaiah will be glad to see to him."

"Are you going to call Riah and London?"

"No, not right now. I want to wait until I know more before I wake them. I just want to keep praying. I can't shake this feeling that this is all my fault, so all I want to do is concentrate on God, His forgiveness, and asking that Isaiah not pay for my sins."

"Jaime," Alonzo said, reaching over to put his hand on my knee. His tone was low-key and sincere. "Now is not the time to start accepting blame for what has happened. We don't even know the entire story. I'm sure there's enough blame to go around. So don't start internalizing this and making it seem like Isaiah's incident is some kind of retribution for something you've done. There's no need to get bogged down with guilt and shame, because we're going to need to surround Isaiah with all the positive energy we can muster. So I say keep praying. Prayer never hurts. But you've repented. God heard it, and from what I know, He's forgiven you. Now you need to seek Him for Isaiah's healing."

"Thanks, Alonzo," I mumbled through tears. I appreciated his comments, but no matter what anybody said, my guilt and my feeling of culpability would not dissipate overnight. It would really take some time. There was no doubt in my mind that if I'd had my family in church, focused on God, and had not neglected my son, this would not have happened.

Although the ride was an hour long, it felt like it took an eternity to get there. The feeling of knowing that something had happened to my child and not being able to be by his side immediately was heart-wrenching. Then, not only was he not in the same state, but I still didn't know the details of what had happened or the severity of the injuries. Alonzo and I were walking into this situation blindly and ignorant to all the facts, which made the situation more excruciating. But, once we made it to the hospital, all of that would change. I planned to be more than informed about my son's condition, how it came to be, and who I could hold responsible for his injuries. However, before heads started to roll, I needed to ensure that my son was all right.

I rushed through the automatic doors of the emergency room. I saw Coach Walker, looking disoriented with red, droopy eyes, like he hadn't slept in a month. I noticed three of Isaiah's teammates sitting in the ER waiting area, as well as some of the other school staff who had accompanied the students.

I ran over to the coach. In a distressed voiced, I said, "Coach Walker, how's Isaiah? What happened?"

Chapter 34

The look on Coach Walker's face alarmed me. He appeared distraught and extremely concerned. Just looking at him gave me an uncomfortable feeling about Isaiah's condition. "Mr. and Mrs. Clarke," he said in a sorrowful tone, "we are still waiting to hear the news about Isaiah. The last I heard he was still in surgery. We're waitin' for the doctor to give us an update."

"Surgery?" I cupped my mouth in shock. "Why does he need surgery?"

"Well, he was . . . he was . . . stabbed tonight."

"What?" Alonzo and I both shrieked.

"Stabbed? Oh, no," I cried. "I gotta find out what's going on with him. I can't take this waiting."

I rushed over to the nurse's station with Alonzo on my heels. "Hi, my name is Jaime Clarke. I'm Isaiah Clarke's mother. I wanna know how he's doing."

"Hold on, let me check," the nurse replied as she immediately got up from her chair and walked in the back. Waiting for her to return felt like I was watching paint dry. I knew she was gone for only a minute or two, but it felt like forever. When she returned, she said, "Ma'am, he just got out of surgery. I informed the doctor that the family is here. He'll be out shortly."

"When can I see him?"

"I'm not sure. The doctor will be able to give you that information," she replied with a weak smile.

"Thanks." I wasn't pleased about not getting immediate answers. Alonzo and I walked back over to where the coach and other school staff were sitting. I noticed that one of Isaiah's teammates sitting in the waiting room was Kyon, Isaiah's weed smoking buddy. He had visible cuts and bruises on his face.

"Coach, please tell me something," I pleaded. "Tell me what happened to Isaiah."

Coach responded, "Let's walk somewhere we can speak privately."

Alonzo and I followed him as we made our way to the opposite side of the waiting room. There, Alonzo and I sat together, and the coach sat in a chair across from us. Looking at us with sadness in his eyes, he said, "First, let me say that I am so sorry this has happened. I know you all entrusted your son's well-being and safety to me, but trust me when I say I had no idea that the kids had left the hotel."

"What do you mean?" Alonzo queried.

"The details are sketchy at this point. All the information I received is from the boys who are sitting over there. I don't know if they are giving me the full story, or if they're not because they are fearful they will get in trouble. But the story as they tell it is this. Someone—nobody is giving me names as to the ringleader—thought it would be a good idea to sneak out of the hotel between ten-thirty and eleven o'clock last night, and go to a club called Club Charm City. Supposedly, the boys found out about a teen night party and wanted to attend. They left the hotel and took a taxi to this nightclub, where they hung out until the lights came on a little before midnight. Once the club closed, the group of boys got into a tiff with another group of boys outside as they were leaving. Apparently, one of these boys accused Kyon of dancing with his girlfriend, and was upset. So, he and

Kyon got into an argument, and they stated that Isaiah and the other boys were trying to remove Kyon from the altercation before it got out of hand. But to the other group of young men it must've seemed like they were going to jump on their friend, and that's when a fight ensued. During the fight, one of the boys must've had a knife, and Isaiah was stabbed during the brawl. Once they saw the blood, the boys ran off. Kyon said the police arrived immediately and called for an ambulance. When the paramedics arrived, they took Isaiah immediately into surgery."

"So when were you notified?" Alonzo asked.

"I got a call from Quintez, another player on the team who'd snuck out to the club. All the students have my cell phone number, and he called my phone, screaming that Isaiah was being taken to the hospital. I asked him what had happened, but he was just too upset for me to get any information from him at that time. So I asked him to put a police officer on the phone, who gave me very brief details of the incident. The police informed me that Isaiah was being rushed to the University of Maryland hospital, and that the other students appeared to be hurt as well, so they too would be transported. I then alerted the other staff members. One agreed to stay behind with the other boys on the team, while the rest of the staff ran downstairs to the hotel lobby, obtained directions to the hospital from someone at the front desk, and jumped in the car. I started making phone calls to parents as we were driving to the hospital."

The tears that fell from my eyes were nonstop. I sat, listening to Coach Walker's account of what happened to Isaiah in horror. My son, after sneaking out of a hotel, roams the streets of Baltimore, an unfamiliar city, gets stabbed supposedly over a girl who had nothing to do with him. Now he was possibly fighting for his life, all because of something so senseless. This couldn't be real. This had to be a dream. I was waiting for someone to smack me to wake me up from this nightmare.

"Mr. and Mrs. Clarke, I'm so sorry. I can't say it enough. Had I known the boys would've thought about sneaking out I would've paired them up with a chaperone. I've never had this happen, never as long as I've been bringing students to Challenge Discovery. I feel so bad about all of this. I really do."

"Coach, it's not your fault. You couldn't have predicted that this would happen," Alonzo said. "Please don't blame yourself for the irrational actions of these teenagers. At this point, all we can do is pray that Isaiah and his friends will be okay."

"Jaime, Alonzo," I heard someone call. I turned to see my mom and dad running over to us. "How's Isaiah?" Mom asked.

"He just got out of surgery. We still don't know anything. We're waiting to speak with the doctor now. All we know is that he was in a fight and was stabbed."

"Oh, dear God," my mother cried out.

"Where was he stabbed?" Dad asked.

"We don't know that, either," Alonzo responded. "We're in the dark. We know nothing, and it's agonizing just waiting here with no answers."

"Mr. and Mrs. Clarke," Coach said, "I'll let you meet with your family. I'm going to go check on the other boys. Their parents should be arriving soon as well."

"Okay, Coach. Thanks," Alonzo said, patting him on his back.

As the coach walked away, Mr. Howard walked up. "Hi, y'all. Any word on Isaiah?"

"No, not yet, Dad." Alonzo sighed.

Mom, being the prayer warrior she was, refused to stand around, waiting for the doctor. "Come on, y'all. We need to band together as a family right now and go to the Lord in prayer. We will pray until the doctor comes. Let's join hands. Bow your heads."

Right there, in the middle of the emergency room waiting area, my mother started seeking the Lord on Isaiah's behalf. She prayed an intense prayer, which included healing for Isaiah, the doctors caring for him, the entire hospital staff, Isaiah's teammates, Coach Walker, the assistant coach, and all the other school personnel. She prayed for strength for Alonzo and me, and that we'd come together in supporting our child, who undoubtedly needed us more than ever. By the end of her prayer, I thought she prayed for everything and everybody with the exception of the florescent white light that shined above us. It was a powerful prayer, and when I opened my eyes and wiped my tears away, I noticed that our circle, which had started off with just Isaiah's five family members, now included his coach, teammates, other parents who had arrived at the hospital, and people in the waiting room we didn't even know. This was a family prayer that truly turned into a cooperative prayer.

In the midst of everyone hugging and drying their eyes after my mom's prayer, the doctor emerged from behind the doubled doors. "Hi, I'm looking for the family of Isaiah Clarke."

Within a nanosecond, I was standing before the doctor. "I'm . . . I'm his mother," I stuttered nervously. My stomach was doing flips, and I didn't think I could handle any bad news. With Alonzo on my right side, holding my hand, and my mom on my left side with her arm around me, I asked, "How is my son?"

"Good morning, ma'am. I'm Dr. Gary Shuron. Your son, Isaiah, is currently in recovery, and the good news is he is going to be all right."

I breathed a heavy sigh of relief. "Oh, thank you, Jesus," I wept. "Thank you."

The same sentiments were expressed by everyone waiting to hear the news.

Dr. Shuron proceeded to tell us about Isaiah's condition. "Your son received penetrating wounds to the chest. Signs of hemorrhagic shock were present when he arrived at the hospital, and radiography revealed left-sided hemothorax."

"What is hemothorax?" Alonzo questioned.

"Hemothorax is basically a condition of blood accumulating in the chest cavity. It's usually traumatic, from a blunt or penetrating injury. So we placed a tube in the left side of his chest. Then he underwent an exploratory laparoscopy, at which a punctured lung injury was diagnosed and repaired. During the surgery, no further significant bleeding was observed, which means the chest tube was draining the blood from his chest effectively."

My dad spoke up to get a clearer understanding, "So, Dr. Shuron, you're basically saying that Isaiah was stabbed in the chest, which caused internal bleeding. To stop the bleeding in his chest cavity, you had to inset a tube to drain the blood. You also had to do surgery to repair his lung that was damaged when he was stabbed."

"Correct," Dr. Shuron replied. "Also, Isaiah's punctured lung is what caused the internal bleeding."

"So, are you sure he's going to be okay?" I asked. "I mean, this isn't life threatening?"

"Let's just say he still needs to recover. Penetrating stab wounds are serious. Isaiah is doing well right now, but we still need to monitor him. He will be in the hospital for at least a week, and then after that, he will need six to eight weeks to recover. So let's just stay positive and hope the worst is over."

"Thank you, Doctor. Can we see him?" I questioned.

"He's in recovery now, so only two may go back to see him right now. After he's admitted, he can have more visitors, but not too many. We need him to get as much rest as he can."

"You've got our word, Dr. Shuron. Isaiah will be in the best care," my dad affirmed.

Alonzo looked over at my dad and agreed with him. "Yes, he will be. With the support of his parents and loving family, he will recover just fine."

As relieved as I was to learn that Isaiah would survive his stab wound, I was still very anxious about going back to the recovery area to see him. I knew seeing him would definitely bring tears to my eyes. I had been crying all night long, but I wanted to remain strong. Isaiah needed me to be strong. For so many months, I had failed him as a mother, so the least I could do for him was to bring positive energy to his bedside.

"Are you ready to go back?" Alonzo asked.

"Yes."

Slowly, Alonzo and I walked side by side, not saying a word, just mentally preparing ourselves to lay eyes upon our son.

Chapter 35

Alonzo and I entered Isaiah's recovery room, where he lay still, peacefully asleep, hooked up to several machines. Silent tears flowed like rivers as I walked to the right side of the hospital bed. I sat down beside his bed and gazed at him. Alonzo solemnly stood on the opposite side of the bed, looking down at Isaiah. I gently grabbed Isaiah's warm hand and put it up against my cheek.

"Isaiah," I softly spoke. "Mommy and Daddy are here. We're right by your side, baby."

Alonzo softly rubbed Isaiah's forehead and said, "You're gonna be fine, champ. The doctor says you can make it through this."

Suddenly, a feeling like no other came over me. I felt chills and goose bumps appeared on my arms. I had an idea who was leading these emotions; I was always taught that when God leads, we should follow. "Alonzo, I think we should pray."

Eagerly, he agreed. Alonzo stretched his arm and extended his hand to me. I grabbed it, and we held hands tightly with our fingers interlocked. We placed our other hands tenderly on Isaiah.

"Dear God, thank you for your loving kindness despite our sins and transgressions. Today, Lord, we just want to give you honor and praise for all the blessings you have bestowed upon us. Although our hearts are distressed at this time, we know that you have all power

in your hands. God, you have witnessed the rebellious-
ness of youth since the very beginning of time. I know
you understand our helplessness over the actions of
our child. Please help Alonzo and me to transform our
fury and frustration into love for each other and for
our child, who has lost his focus. Lord, come into our
hearts and mind, and share your loving wisdom with
us on how to be more loving and wise parents. Help us
begin to repair our broken fences and heal our broken
hearts. Bless our child, and also help him mend the
error of his ways. In your Word, it says in Psalm 25:7,
'Remember not the sins of my youth, nor my transgressions; according to thy mercy remember thou me for
thy goodness' sake, O Lord.' Help and bless us all to do
right in your name, and restore us to peace and tranquility. Lord, Isaiah is your child first, and you love him
as you love all your children. We ask that you please
bring healing to him, as he is not well. Stay by his side,
and comfort him through this trying time. And, Lord,
while you're curing Isaiah of his physical and emotional wounds, please bless Alonzo and me with your
powerful healing and comfort as well. Thank you for
hearing our prayer. In Jesus' precious name, Amen."

"Amen," Alonzo said as he squeezed my hand.

My tears continued to flow, but a peace that sur-
passed all understanding engulfed me. I wasn't worried. I just knew in my heart that God had heard my
emotional plea, and that He was going to fix it.

As we sat at Isaiah's bedside, I just stared at my child
and stroked his face. Alonzo sat quietly for a few minutes, appearing to be deep in thought. Then, he finally
broke his silence.

"Jaime, we can't go back to living the way we have
over the past few months. It's not healthy for you or
me, and definitely not for Isaiah. I have made some

mistakes. You have made some mistakes. Isaiah has made his share of mistakes. But, for some reason, as much as it hurts to see our son lying in this hospital, I don't think this incident was a mistake."

"What do you mean?" I asked, confused.

"Sure, it was wrong for Isaiah to sneak out of the hotel, but I believe it was all in the plans. He had been crying out for help for months, and we did a poor job of addressing his needs. This stabbing was a wake-up call—for *all* of us. You and I need to decide if we are gonna stick this thing out and work on our marriage and our family, or go our separate ways. But this hurt inflicted upon one another isn't benefiting anybody. Now even with all that has happened tonight, I don't want to give up on my family." Alonzo's eyes became a little misty. I could tell he was fighting back tears as he continued to speak. "As I sit here and look at Isaiah and look across at you, I realize that if I ever lost either of you, I'd be devastated. I want to fight for my family, but only if you're sincerely willing to do so."

Tears, along with mucus from my nose, covered my face. I was truly touched by Alonzo's words. For the first time in a long time, I believed every single word that came out of his mouth. I felt God moving already. The Lord was omnipresent, and He had definitely shown Himself in Isaiah's hospital room.

"I agree," I responded. "It's time to make our family whole again. I vow to you today that there will be no more acts of revenge on my part."

I wasn't sure how much Isaiah could hear, so I waved for Alonzo to walk over to the door of Isaiah's hospital room so we could finish our conversation. I didn't want him to learn that I, too, had been unfaithful. I felt more comfortable speaking to Alonzo on the other side of the room rather than sitting at Isaiah's bedside.

I looked deeply into Alonzo's eyes and whispered, "No more hurt, no more lies, no more relationships outside this martial union. I love you, Alonzo, and I know the pain I caused isn't what love is supposed to look and feel like. We owe it to ourselves and to Isaiah to grow up and start being more responsible, respectable adults."

"Jaime, I'll admit," he whispered, "I was devastated to learn about the encounters with two different men. I never expected this from you, and, quite frankly, I don't think I could stomach any more details. Getting a taste of my own medicine was an eye-opening experience for me. No doubt I was hurt and crushed. I'm still messed up in the head about it. However, this revelation was a clear sign that we need to work on our issues in a major way. If anything, I want to battle anyone and everyone to save us, to save our family. Now, I don't know where to start this healing process, but I'd like to suggest finding a new church home and starting family therapy."

Through my snot and tears, I managed a weak smile. "I think that's a great idea. I think therapy will began to help us work toward forgiveness and learn to trust each other again. I'm excited about the idea already."

Alonzo walked over to me and held out his arms. "May I have a hug?"

I didn't verbally respond to his request. I just fell into his arms and squeezed him tightly.

"I love you, Jaime. I really do."

"I love you too, Alonzo."

As I stood in Alonzo's arms, we heard a moan. We jumped. We turned to look at Isaiah. His eyes were open. We rushed over to his bedside.

"Hi, baby. Mommy and Daddy are here with you."

He didn't speak, but his big, brown eyes were smiling. I surmised that he must have felt the outpouring of love between his mother and father flowing in the atmosphere of his room. This emotion undoubtedly made his heart glad—a feeling he hadn't felt in months.

Chapter 36

Finally, after a weeklong stay in the hospital, Isaiah had been released to go home, but not without strict instructions from Dr. Shuron. He would stay home for the next six weeks: the first two on bed rest, and the remaining weeks with very light activities, such as walking up and down stairs, bathing, and things of that nature. Alonzo hired a nurse to come into our home to help take care of Isaiah. He would need his wounds cleaned and bandages changed, and we weren't confident about whether we'd do a great job with home health care. Alonzo arranged for the nurse to be at our home when we arrived back in Virginia.

Alonzo also made follow-up appointments with Isaiah's regular physician through Inova Fairfax Hospital, and planned for him to be homeschooled for the remainder of the school year. Alonzo had been great, taking the necessary steps to get things in order for Isaiah's arrival home.

It had been an eventful week. I never left the hospital, but Alonzo did travel back to Virginia to bring clothing and toiletries for me. Riah, London, Everett, and Nick traveled to Baltimore to visit Isaiah. And the best news of all was that the Baltimore City Police Department had come to the hospital to notify us that they were able to apprehend three of the teenagers involved in the brawl and the stabbing. The young man who stabbed Isaiah was only sixteen years old. It broke my heart that these young African American males would involve themselves in such senseless acts, like sneaking out of the hotel to go to a club, as well as the other boys who wanted to fight over a girl and resort to violence with no regard for human life.

Just as we pulled into the driveway of our home, Isaiah, who had been quiet for most the ride, said, "Ma, Dad. I'm sorry. I know you've heard me say this before, but I really mean it. It was a stupid idea to sneak out of the hotel that night and go to the club. Had I not done that, I wouldn't have gotten into that fight. I made a dumb mistake, and now I'm paying the price for it. I promise you, I have learned my lesson. I'm gonna do better. I promise, I will." Isaiah's voice cracked a little. I could hear the sincerity in his voice. I think the attack scared him. It was not only a wake-up call for Alonzo and me, but a hard lesson learned for him as well.

"Son," Alonzo said, "you used poor judgment that night, and I'm glad to hear that you've learned from this experience. We accept your apology, and we'll discuss this further once your health improves, but right now our focus is getting you healthy again. We love you unconditionally, Isaiah, and we're just glad to be able to bring you home today."

I turned around to look at Isaiah in the back seat. He looked really remorseful. "Your dad is right. We love you, and nothing you can do will change that. Now, let's get you in the house and get you comfortable."

Alonzo helped Isaiah from the car and up the sidewalk to our front door. I went ahead of them to open the front door. As Alonzo helped Isaiah inside the house, he was greeted by family and friends.

"Welcome home, Isaiah," they shouted as he entered the house. He beamed, as he was pleasantly surprised to see his grandparents; his cousins London, Nick, and Gabriel; and Riah and Everett. His nurse quickly ran to Isaiah's side to assist Alonzo with getting him seated on the living room sofa.

"Hi, everybody," Isaiah said.

"How's my grandson?" Mr. Howard asked.

"I'm doing much better. I still have some pains, but the doctor gave me some medicine."

"Well, you make sure you take your meds and get plenty of rest. Gotta get you out of this house and back to a Wizards game before the season ends."

Isaiah laughed. "That sounds great, Granddad."

While Isaiah continued to chitchat with his visitors, I moseyed into the kitchen to see what my mom had been cooking. It smelled like a soul food restaurant when I walked into the house. It had been so long since I'd had a home-cooked meal. I was anxious to dig into Mom's pots and pans.

"Hey, Mom, whatcha cooking?"

"Jaime, I figured you and Alonzo would have your hands full with Isaiah all week and wouldn't have much time to cook, so I fixed a few different dishes—ham, barbeque chicken, pot roast along with collard greens, macaroni and cheese, and potato salad. That way, all you have to do is warm up food. I also went grocery shopping and stocked up on luncheon meat, bread, chips, and meals to pop in the microwave, too."

I kissed Mom on her cheek. "Thanks. You're the greatest."

"You're welcome, sweetie. But it's not just me. Howard brought homemade chicken noodle soup for Isaiah. London cooked string beans and Riah made rotisserie chicken. Everett and Nick stocked the house with beverages, so it was truly a group effort."

"Wow. I had no idea." I got a little teary-eyed. "I appreciate y'all more than you'll know."

"We're family. That's what we do." Mom smiled.

After chatting with Mom, I went back into the living room to check on Isaiah. "Hey, honey. Would you like something to eat?"

"I'm okay, Ma. I think I'm ready to go upstairs to lie down."

I thought the drive from Baltimore and visiting with the family probably tired Isaiah out. Alonzo and my dad helped him upstairs to his bedroom. It seemed like Isaiah's incident not only helped his dad and me to see the error of our ways, but I noticed that my dad's heart had softened toward Alonzo. He was treating him like "his son" again.

While the men assisted Isaiah upstairs with the nurse behind them, I took a moment to share some news with Mom, London, and Riah. When I pulled them into the kitchen, Riah grinned. "What? What's going on? What are you being sneaky about?"

"I'm not being sneaky," I whispered. "I just wanted y'all to know that Alonzo asked if we could go to counseling. He said he really wants to save our marriage."

"Praise the Lord," Mom exclaimed.

"Shh." I laughed. "When we were in the hospital with Isaiah, we realized that we'd both made some serious mistakes," I said as I eyed Riah. She was the only one in the room who knew exactly what my mistakes were. "So, he said he wants to find a new church home and start family therapy."

"That's wonderful," London emphasized as she gave me a big hug.

"I'm happy for you, Jaime." Riah smiled. "Initially, I was all for you going your separate ways, but I know you love him, and I want you to make this work."

"I just wanted to thank you all for the love, support, and encouragement you've given me over these past few months. It's been rough with Alonzo, Isaiah, and my health. It's been a rough ride, but I am blessed to be surrounded by a wonderful group of people who love and care for me. I couldn't have made it through this trying ordeal without y'all."

"Aw," Riah said. "You know we'd do anything for you." She, too, leaned in to give me a hug. But as we embraced, she whispered in my ear. "Did you take care of that other situation?"

"Yes and no," I replied. I knew my answer was ambiguous, but I didn't have time to go into details. She'd just have to accept that I would fill her in later.

Just as Riah was about to form her lips to question me further, the door bell rang. *Saved by the bell,* I thought as I dashed out of the kitchen to answer the door.

When I opened the door, I recoiled. I was startled. I couldn't believe my eyes. I just knew they were playing tricks on me.

"What are you doing here?" I whispered. It was Mario. In the flesh, standing at my front door.

"I came to check on you. I've been worried. The last message I got from you said that your husband had found out about us and that your son was in the hospital. I've been calling your cell phone, texting you, and I haven't heard a word. I didn't know if you were dead or alive. So I had to take my chances and come see you for myself."

I pushed Mario away from my front door and closed it behind me. I pulled him down the sidewalk and into the driveway. "Are you trying to get me killed? Why would you show up here?"

"That's just it. When I didn't hear from you in all this time, I didn't know if your husband had done something to you. I didn't know if Isaiah was in the hospital as a result of Alonzo finding out about us. I ain't know shit. I was concerned."

"You gotta go. I appreciate your concern, but you are wrong to come to my house."

"I feel you, Jaime, and I'll leave now, but I needed to know that you were all right. I needed to see your pretty face for myself."

"I appreciate your concern about me, but you have to know that showing up at my door was not the best way to express your concern. But, since you're here, I need to tell you that in light of everything that's happened, we can't see each other anymore. Alonzo found out about me being with you, and right before we got the phone call about Isaiah we were in a heated argument. Isaiah's accident was a frightening, yet eye-opening, experience. I realized that I can't keep living such a sinful lifestyle. I promised God that if He saved my baby's life, I would turn away from sin, and I want to do that."

I could see sadness spread across Mario's face. "I understand."

"You were a good friend to me, Mario. I just wanted you to know that I am grateful for your friendship, but I need to focus on my marriage, my son, my health, and rededicating my life to God."

"I had many fun times with you, Jaime. I'll miss you, but I agree you should put family first."

Just as Mario and I were about to say our final good-byes, Alonzo shouted my name. "Jaime! Jaime!" he said as he rushed to my side.

I thought I felt my bowels loosen within my body at the sound of Alonzo's voice. I was nervous as hell. Mario and Alonzo were standing face-to-face. I hoped that a UFO would swoop in at anytime and removed me from this uncomfortable situation.

"Who is this?" Alonzo growled.

"Alonzo," I said, grabbing his arm gently, "calm down. It's not what you think."

"I'm gonna ask again," he said, giving Mario a hard stare. There was no doubt he recognized him from the cell phone picture that was sent to him the night we attended the swingers' party. I was sure Mario's face was one he'd never forget.

"I'm Mario." He spoke matter-of-factly, with no appearance of being intimidated by Alonzo.

"You must be out your mind to even think it's okay to be standing in front of my home after you've been sleeping with my wife. Tell me why I shouldn't put your ass in a comatose state right now."

I wrapped my arms around Alonzo's waist and held him tightly in an attempt to restrain him. "Alonzo, he was just leaving," I said nervously. "I told him that it's over between us. That we were working on rebuilding our family. He understands and respects it."

"Look, I'm not here to start any trouble," Mario interjected. "I'll admit, I care more about Jaime than I realized, and when I hadn't heard from her for a few days, I was concerned. I mean no disrespect, but I just wanted to ensure that she was okay."

"She's not your concern. Never has been and never will be. She's my wife. I'll take care of her, not you. Now, you've had your time with *my* wife, but that bogus relationship is over and done. I'm pissed the hell off about it, and the fact that you've got the gall to come to my house makes me even more irate, but I'm gonna chalk that up to you being naive and stupid."

"I'm not—" Mario stammered, but his thought was cut short.

"I'm not done talking," Alonzo bellowed. He walked closer to Mario and stood directly in his face. Mario didn't flinch, but I continued to hold on to Alonzo securely just in case he got the urge to attack Mario.

"You had your li'l fling with Jaime and, although it sickens me, I'm willing to move on and forgive. But let me warn you right now; don't you ever, ever, in your life, put your hands on my wife again. Do not call her, don't text her, don't e-mail her, don't ever come to our house, and don't even think about her. If I find out that you've communicated with her in any way, there will be hell to pay."

Mario threw up his hands and began to back away from Alonzo. "Hey, man, you don't have to worry about me. It's over between us. I have no problems respecting the two of you wanting to repair your marriage. I will not stand in the way of that."

"Good. Now you can bounce up off my property," Alonzo ordered.

Mario didn't say another word. He turned away and walked toward his car.

"I'm sorry, Alonzo. I had no idea he was coming here. I'm sorry."

"Yeah, well, he better make this his one and only visit. If there is a next time, I won't be so nice."

After Mario sped away, Alonzo and I walked back toward the house. I had no idea how this little episode would affect the rest of our evening, but I felt some chilly vibes coming from him.

When we walked back into the house, Riah and London whisked me into the kitchen.

"Who was that?" Riah questioned anxiously.

"What was going on outside?" London asked.

In a sullen tone, I responded, "Nothing I can get into right now. I'll tell you later."

"All right, but I'm gonna call you when I get home," Riah said, as she must have had an inkling it had something to do with my affair.

It was my hope that neither London nor Riah would follow up with me later regarding the scene outside, because I didn't want to rehash it. I had officially closed that chapter of my life. It was done and I didn't see the benefit of discussing it. My time would be better served repairing my marriage and nursing Isaiah back to good health.

I left the kitchen to escape any further interrogation from Riah and London. I walked into the living room to chat with Alonzo. When we'd come back into the house, he immediately went upstairs to check on Isaiah, so I wasn't sure what kind of mood he was in after his encounter with Mario. I took this opportunity to feel him out a bit, to determine his demeanor.

"Was everything okay with Isaiah while you were there?" I asked Alonzo.

"Yeah, he's fine. He's resting."

"Does he still not want anything to eat?"

"Naw. I think he just wants to take it easy. Besides, I think the pain medication makes him drowsy. He'll probably be drifting off to sleep soon."

"I'm gonna go check on him."

Alonzo appeared to be pretty pleasant. I hoped this wasn't an act for our guests.

Still feeling quite uneasy about the confrontation and the consequences that may be in store, I quietly left the crowd of family members chatting in the living room and went to bathroom in the master bedroom.

I closed the door and locked it. I turned on the cold water in the sink and let it run. I walked over the toilet and sat on the closed lid. I closed my eyes and silently prayed.

A few moments into my meditation, I was summoned. "Jaime, where are you?" It was Alonzo.

"I'm in the bathroom," I yelled through the door. "I'll be out in a minute."

I flushed the toilet, rinsed my hands under the cold, running water, and dried them. When I opened the door, Alonzo was standing right there.

"I was wondering where you were. Everybody's getting ready to leave, and they want to say their goodbyes."

"Okay. I'll be right down. But wait, may I ask you something?

"What's up?" he asked.

"Are you angry with me about what happened earlier?"

"I can't say that I'm happy. I'm still quite miffed that dude had the balls to show up at our house. I keep thinking of all the things I should've said to him while we were standing face–to-face. I ain't gonna lie. It will take a long minute to digest this whole ordeal."

"You have to know that I had nothing to do with him coming here, right?" I sincerely asked.

"Oh, I know you didn't."

"All I can say is I'm sorry. I'm so sorry. I just hope this doesn't change your mind about working on our marriage and our family."

"Never that. I told you I'm committed to us and I mean that. I'm not gonna let that punk change that. But you have to promise me that today was your last time communicating with him. It's gotta be done, Jaime. Done."

"I swear to you it's over."

"Cool. Then let's go say adios to the fam." He reached out for my hand and we walked downstairs to express our sincere thanks for everyone coming over and to say farewell.

"Mr. Howard, are you leaving already?" I said after Alonzo and I rejoined everyone.

"Yes, baby girl," he said, giving me a side hug. "I want you all to get some rest."

"Well, thanks so much for the soup."

"No problem. I'll call later to check on you all."

He hugged Alonzo, waved to everyone else, and left.

Next London, Nick, and Gabriel gave their farewell. "See ya, cuz. I'll be back over tomorrow. Call us if you need anything."

I hugged and kissed her, thanked them for cooking for us, and promised I would call if I needed anything.

I turned to see Riah and Everett about to make their exit. "You all are leaving too?"

"Yes. This is your first day back in your home. Go upstairs and lie across your bed. You all will have your hands full taking care of Isaiah, so make sure you get plenty of rest. I'll call you this evening."

"Okay. Thank you all for the food and the drinks," I said as we embraced. I then whispered in Riah's ear, "It's done—completely done." Riah looked at me and winked.

I smiled at my parents as they walked downstairs from saying their good-byes to Isaiah. I knew it was pretty difficult for them to see their grandson, the child they helped raise, lying in bed recovering from a stab wound.

"How is he?" I asked.

"He's still sleeping," Mom responded. "We just quietly kissed him and told him we'd see him tomorrow."

"Good. He'll be glad to see you all. Oh and, Mom, thanks so much for preparing the meals for us. We have so much food I won't have to cook until next week." I hugged my parents. "Love you, Mom and Dad."

"Love you too," they said in unison.

My dad turned to me and said, "Your mother told me that you and Alonzo are seeking counseling."

"Yes, Dad."

"I think that's a good idea. I know that you've had your problems lately, but this is a family worth saving. Whatever your mother and I can do to help, just ask. We're here for emotional support and anything else you need to help make your lives better."

"Aw, thanks, Dad. You guys have already done so much. Alonzo and I can't thank you enough for being there for us through the good times and the not-so-good times."

"And, Mom and Dad, I know I disappointed you, but I promise to make things right," Alonzo added. "I'm striving to be the man God intended me to be, and I just ask that you all continue to pray for us."

Mom walked over and kissed Alonzo gently on his cheek. "You're not a perfect person. None of us are. You and Jaime both have your flaws, but keep God first and in the center of your household, and you can never go wrong. We will continue to uplift you in prayer, and know that you, Jaime, and Isaiah will always have our love and support."

As my parents headed toward the door, my dad turned to Alonzo and shook his hand. "Please take care of your family."

Looking my dad directly in the eye, Alonzo responded, "I will, sir. I will."

For the first time in weeks, I had an overwhelming feeling of peace and tranquility. My stomach wasn't hurting. My mind was free from negativity. I didn't feel depressed. I wasn't crying. I wasn't worried about anything. I was just in a state of serenity. Of course, not all was perfect in the Clarke household. There were many issues we needed to work on, but I felt that, as a family, we were finally moving forward, striving for happiness.

Epilogue

Two months later

Praise God! Isaiah was finally given a clean bill of health and allowed to resume all activities. The last two months had not been easy for him, having to stay confined to the house. He had an excellent home school teacher who came to our house every day to ensure he didn't fall behind in his academics. He also participated in the state standardized testing at the end of the school year. When his final report card came, Isaiah had once again made the honor roll with mostly A's and one B. We were pleased. Now, with the school year behind us and the summer upon us, we were still making strides to improve our family. We were embarking upon our first family therapy session, and I was looking forward to it.

Alonzo had done some extensive research and found a therapist, Dr. Montana Saxby, who specialized in psychotherapy that involved treating all members of the nuclear family collectively and individually.

When we arrived at the office, we were greeted by Dr. Saxby, an African American woman who looked to be in her mid-forties. She had honey-colored skin, with naturally curly, brown hair. She was very pleasant and seemed enthusiastic about our visit.

"Please come in and have a seat," she said as we entered her office. It was a huge, executive-like office that had a living room appeal with a couch, love seat, end tables, and hanging plants. Alonzo, Isaiah, and I sat on the coach.

"We're happy to be here, Dr. Saxby," I said. "My name is Jaime, this is my husband, Alonzo, and our son, Isaiah."

"Nice meeting you all. You're a great-looking family."

"Thank you," we responded.

"So, with this being our first meeting, this will be more of an information gathering session. I'll find out a little about you, your backgrounds, and then I'll explain to you how family therapy works. Let us begin with one of you telling me why you're here today seeking counseling."

Before today's session, Alonzo and I had discussed how open we'd be in front of Isaiah about the problems in our marriage. Although this was therapy for the family, we agreed there were certain things about our relationship we didn't need to expose to him. We hoped Dr. Saxby would understand that and not push too hard.

Alonzo cleared his throat. "Dr. Saxby, it's probably too involved to sum up in a few sentences, but, in a nutshell, we're here today because we'd like to improve how we function as a family and our home environment. I think we have difficulties with communicating effectively and problem solving. Overall, we would like to create a better functioning home environment."

"How long have you been having the problems that you've described?" Dr. Saxby inquired.

"Jaime and I have had ups and downs in our relationship for a while now, but our greatest difficulties hit us in the beginning of this year—around January and February."

"And what was that?"

Alonzo sighed. I knew he didn't want to get into great detail in front of Isaiah, and, quite frankly, I didn't want him to either. He had already been exposed to more of our foolishness than he should have been. "Well, Doctor, I take responsibly for the downfall of our family. I did some things I'm not proud of, and, as a result, I not only hurt my wife, but my son was affected in the process. As much as we tried as a family to bounce back from it, we couldn't, and things just got increasingly out of control."

"Also," I interjected, not wanting Alonzo to take total blame, "the way I dealt with my anguish contributed to the problems in the family. I blame myself for a lot of what happened to Isaiah. Had I not been caught up in my own emotions and been in tune to what our son was dealing with, maybe he wouldn't have been acting out the way he did."

Dr. Saxby turned to Isaiah. "What kind of problems have you had, Isaiah?" she asked gently.

Isaiah's eyes were glued to the floor. I could tell he was uncomfortable, but all of us were experiencing feelings of uneasiness. In order for us to establish a healthy family environment, we had to go through the tough stuff first, and this was one of those times.

Fiddling with his fingers, Isaiah said, "My grades dropped in school. I used to get all As and made honor roll, but then I barely made Cs. I got caught smoking weed and drinking alcohol. The worst thing I did was sneak out of the hotel room on a school trip and go to a club. At the club, me and my friends got into a fight, and I got stabbed."

"Oh, wow. I'm sorry to hear that. It does seem like you've had a tough time. Would you say that these things had anything to do with the problems between your mom and dad?" the therapist asked.

Isaiah looked afraid to answer. I put my hand on his knee and said, "It's okay, baby. You can tell her the truth."

"Um . . . yeah. I hated what was happening with them. Sometimes it made me mad and sometimes I was sad. The house always seemed unhappy—nobody around me was happy, and I hated hearing them argue."

"Thank you so much for expressing your feelings, Isaiah. I know that wasn't easy for you, but you did a great job," Dr. Saxby encouraged him. "Okay, well, I think we're off to a good start. I'd like to speak to each of you individually, but before I do, let me explain a little bit of the process of family therapy. Let me warn you that I am not going to wave a magic wand and all your problems will disappear. I wish that were the case, but it's not. It will take work on each of your parts. You will need to be fully committed to the process of change. Some sessions will be with all three of you, and then some of them may be just two of you, or I may request an individual session. Also, we will engage in some role-playing, and I will give you assignments to take home. As your therapist, I will develop a family treatment plan that addresses the greatest needs of your family. One issue that immediately sticks out is the need to improve the way you relate to each other. So I want to enhance your capacity to deal with the content of your problems, manage conflict in an appropriate manner, and by and large improve the family dynamic. Would you all agree?"

"Yes," Alonzo and I responded.

"I also would like to spend some quality time with the two of you," Dr. Saxby said, pointing to Alonzo and me. "I think if we get to the root of your marital issues and mend them, it would be beneficial to the family."

"I wholeheartedly agree, Doctor," I said. "I think Isaiah's problems came about because of the problems in our marriage. I think our venom and rage spilled over to him."

"Good assessment, Jaime," Dr. Saxby said. "I would also like to spend some individual time with you. I see on the paperwork you've listed that you have Crohn's disease."

"Yes, I do."

"As you may know, the last thing you need when suffering from Crohn's disease is stress. So I'd like to work with you on stress management techniques and some other things."

"Thanks so much. I'm in desperate need of any techniques that will help me manage stress."

"Okay, so the next thing I'd like to do is meet with Isaiah alone, and then I'll meet with the two of you individually."

Alonzo and I left the office and walked toward the waiting area. When we sat down, Alonzo reached over to grab my hand. "I have a good feeling about this," he said. "I'm glad we made this step to better our family."

"Yes, me too." I smiled. "I just want to thank you for agreeing to come to counseling. You know most black men won't commit to therapy. It's a taboo subject."

Alonzo laughed. "Yeah, it is, but no other black man has as beautiful a wife and intelligent a son, both worth fighting for. I mean it when I say my past is my past. My focus is God, you, and Isaiah—that's it."

I squeezed Alonzo's hand, and then I leaned over and tenderly kissed his lips. "I love you, Alonzo. I'm looking forward to our fresh start."

"I love you more, Jaime Clarke, and I, too, am ready for new a beginning."

Hand in hand, we sat quietly, taking in the moment. Life was good. I took a moment to reflect on the past six months. The whole ordeal had started with Pastor Steele's scandal. That was the beginning of all our trials, and while I, a faithful member of Sprit of Truth for so many years, suffered because of his salacious acts, he was still preaching to the masses. It was business as usual at that church, and although I was disgusted that he was still preaching the Word of God, I prayed for the naive souls who remained under his leadership.

While the flock at Spirit of Truth had to endure the likes of Pastor Steele, my family and I had found a place of worship, which was named, appropriately, Family Worship Center. Someday we may call this place our church home. Because I still had some trust issues concerning church and pastors, I decided not to rush to become a member, but every Sunday after church, Alonzo, Isaiah, and I would discuss how much we enjoyed the service, the various ministries, community involvement, and most of all a pastor who preached the Gospel according to the Bible and not his own interpretation.

Candice Barr was finally history. After wreaking havoc for so many weeks, the restraining order finally kept her quiet. It was so wonderful to not have to deal with her antics anymore, and I prayed it stayed that way.

I still had no contact with Mario. I meant it when I said it was over. My focus was on Alonzo and Isaiah and my health. Not surprisingly, once I stopped drinking excessively, the Crohn's disease symptoms decreased. I hoped that it wouldn't take long to go into remission.

Overall, it had been a tumultuous first half of the year for Alonzo, Isaiah, and me, and although all our issues hadn't been resolved, we were determined more than ever to strengthen our family unit. With God's grace we made it through a six-month storm, and with God's infinite wisdom, I knew that the Clarke family would, without a doubt, be victorious and made whole.

Notes

Notes

ORDER FORM
URBAN BOOKS, LLC
78 E. Industry Ct
Deer Park, NY 11729

Name: (please print): _____

Address: _____

City/State: _____

Zip: _____

QTY	TITLES	PRICE
	16 On The Block	$14.95
	A Girl From Flint	$14.95
	A Pimp's Life	$14.95
	Baltimore Chronicles	$14.95
	Baltimore Chronicles 2	$14.95
	Betrayal	$14.95
	Black Diamond	$14.95
	Black Diamond 2	$14.95
	Black Friday	$14.95
	Both Sides Of The Fence	$14.95
	Both Sides Of The Fence 2	$14.95
	California Connection	$14.95

Shipping and handling-add $3.50 for 1st book, then $1.75 for each additional book.

Please send a check payable to:

Urban Books, LLC

Please allow 4-6 weeks for delivery

ORDER FORM
URBAN BOOKS, LLC
78 E. Industry Ct
Deer Park, NY 11729

Name: (please print):_____

Address: _____

City/State: _____

Zip: _____

QTY	TITLES	PRICE
	California Connection 2	$14.95
	Cheesecake And Teardrops	$14.95
	Congratulations	$14.95
	Crazy In Love	$14.95
	Cyber Case	$14.95
	Denim Diaries	$14.95
	Diary Of A Mad First Lady	$14.95
	Diary Of A Stalker	$14.95
	Diary Of A Street Diva	$14.95
	Diary Of A Young Girl	$14.95
	Dirty Money	$14.95
	Dirty To The Grave	$14.95

Shipping and handling-add $3.50 for 1st book, then $1.75 for each additional book.

Please send a check payable to:
Urban Books, LLC
Please allow 4-6 weeks for delivery

ORDER FORM
URBAN BOOKS, LLC
78 E. Industry Ct
Deer Park, NY 11729

Name:(please print):_____

Address: _____

City/State: _____

Zip: _____

QTY	TITLES	PRICE
	Gunz And Roses	$14.95
	Happily Ever Now	$14.95
	Hell Has No Fury	$14.95
	Hush	$14.95
	If It Isn't love	$14.95
	Kiss Kiss Bang Bang	$14.95
	Last Breath	$14.95
	Little Black Girl Lost	$14.95
	Little Black Girl Lost 2	$14.95
	Little Black Girl Lost 3	$14.95
	Little Black Girl Lost 4	$14.95
	Little Black Girl Lost 5	$14.95

Shipping and handling-add $3.50 for 1st book, then $1.75 for each additional book.
Please send a check payable to:
     Urban Books, LLC
Please allow 4-6 weeks for delivery

ORDER FORM
URBAN BOOKS, LLC
78 E. Industry Ct
Deer Park, NY 11729

Name: (please print):_____

Address: _____

City/State: _____

Zip: _____

QTY	TITLES	PRICE
	Loving Dasia	$14.95
	Material Girl	$14.95
	Moth To A Flame	$14.95
	Mr. High Maintenance	$14.95
	My Little Secret	$14.95
	Naughty	$14.95
	Naughty 2	$14.95
	Naughty 3	$14.95
	Queen Bee	$14.95
	Say It Ain't So	$14.95
	Snapped	$14.95
	Snow White	$14.95

Shipping and handling-add $3.50 for 1st book, then $1.75 for each additional book.
Please send a check payable to:
Urban Books, LLC
Please allow 4-6 weeks for delivery

ORDER FORM
URBAN BOOKS, LLC
78 E. Industry Ct
Deer Park, NY 11729

Name: (please print): _____

Address: _____

City/State: _____

Zip: _____

QTY	TITLES	PRICE
	Spoil Rotten	$14.95
	Supreme Clientele	$14.95
	The Cartel	$14.95
	The Cartel 2	$14.95
	The Cartel 3	$14.95
	The Dopefiend	$14.95
	The Dopeman Wife	$14.95
	The Prada Plan	$14.95
	The Prada Plan 2	$14.95
	Where There Is Smoke	$14.95
	Where There Is Smoke 2	$14.95

Shipping and handling-add $3.50 for 1st book, then $1.75 for each additional book.

Please send a check payable to:

Urban Books, LLC

Please allow 4-6 weeks for delivery